Laurel Lake Lodge

ISBN 978-1-989642-49-8 (paperback)
ISBN 978-1-989642-54-2 (ebook)
Laurel Lake Lodge © 2025 Lintusen Press. Shawn L. Bird, editor.

This is a collaborative novel project. The authors below share copyright of this book. Authors contributed scenes primarily connected to the following characters:

Alison McBain (Daphne, Betsy), Chris McMahen (Darren, Leeroy), Shawn L. Bird (compiler), Mandy Eve Barnett (Yize Peng), Isabel Cave (Grace), J. L. G. Dufort (Jonathan), Anna Keet (Leo), Dianne Koebel-Pede (Maxine), Kathleen Ladislaus (Scout), Shannon Lalonde (Molly), Elim Ng (Celina), Stephen Ullstrom (Duke), and Trevor Vestad (Alistar).

Original cover design by Lintusen Press with images and features under license from Canva Pro. Used with permission.

This book uses Canadian English.

Lintusen Press
PO Box 10019 Salmon Arm BC V1E 3B9

LINTUSEN PRESS
PRESENTS

Laurel Lake Lodge

ABOUT THIS BOOK

This is a collaborative novel. It began as a brainstorm with about sixty people in a workshop presented by Shawn Bird at Calgary's When Words Collide Writers' Conference in August, 2024.

Over the next few months, the writers who chose to commit to the project worked on a communal document online to flesh out the characters and plot lines generated at the workshop and to write the chapters and scenes.

When the first drafts of the chapters were completed, the project passed back to Shawn who endeavoured to meld the disparate elements into a cohesive story.

What an adventure!

The authors were primary champions of the following character(s):

- Alison McBain   Daphne, Betsy
- Chris McMahen   Leeroy, Darren Jr.
- Shawn L. Bird   compiler
- Mandy Eve Barnett   Yize
- Isabel Cave   Grace
- J. L. G. Dufort   Jonathan
- Anna Keet   Leo
- Dianne Koebel-Pede   Maxine
- Kathleen Ladislaus   Scout
- Shannon Lalonde   Molly
- Elim Ng   Celina
- Stephen Ullstrom   Duke
- Trevor Vestad   Alistar

1.
Coming Home

Daphne Laurel

The last time Daphne had walked through the door of Laurel Lake Lodge was the time she'd vowed never to return, following the big, blowout argument when she'd told her dad that he might as well already be dead if he couldn't let the past stay in the past.

Now, she felt like she'd just hopped aboard a time machine and gone back to that pivotal moment. Nothing seemed to have changed about the place. If anything, Laurel Lake Lodge had only gotten worse. The front porch was sagging and looked as if one or two of the boards were in the process of rotting through. The paint was peeling along the walls, and a few windows were missing shutters. There were lighter-colored rectangles where the shutters used to be.

All in all, the Lodge was a dump. Or, at least, more of a dump than when she'd left. She was not just shocked that basic upkeep hadn't been maintained, but that it seemed her dad had let the place fall apart in so many other ways. Why anyone would book a stay here was beyond her.

The woman behind the front desk glanced up as the bell over the door dinged. "Welcome to Laurel Lodge—" She paused, her jaw dropping open. "Holy, hell, is it . . .? It is!

Daphne Laurel, as I live and breathe. What are you doing back here?"

Daphne probably should have braced herself for a familiar face or two. However, she hadn't expected to see Grace Taylor right away. Grace was the daughter of Laurel Lake Lodge's longtime housekeeper, Louise. But what was she doing behind the front desk now? That was a new development.

"Oh, good to see you," Daphne said noncommittally, dodging Grace's question. "Is Dad in?"

"Is your dad—well, of course he's in! Let me go get him. Wait here a second."

Before Daphne could protest, which was her automatic reaction, Grace had disappeared down the back corridor. Daphne wasn't sure why she would want to protest, though, other than the fact it felt weird being treated as a guest in the building where she'd grown up. Had she been gone so long that she no longer belonged here?

But she was here for a reason. She had a mission: a message needed to be delivered. There was only so long that she could ignore the deadline hanging over her head. She'd finally decided that she had to come back to Laurel Lake—it was important to do this in person.

Besides, her father might just have hung up on her if she'd called. She had no idea. It had been months since they'd spoken, and often the conversation seemed to turn to the same things—what he called her "so-called career" in hospitality services. "Bah, 'hospitality' is just a fancy name for running a hotel," he'd griped more than once.

She didn't remind him that she'd gone to school for it, and gotten a double major in business and marketing too. Then she spent years working for various hotels large and small, including boutique ones that were in much better shape than Laurel Lake Lodge.

Her practiced eye ran over the lobby. The carpets were clean, but worn. They could use replacing. They were threadbare in places. The banister railing going upstairs looked rickety. Someone gripping it too hard might take it down. Did her father not understand this was a safety hazard? To top it all off, there was peeling paint inside and outside. She noticed a few patches near the bottoms of the windows that looked suspiciously damp.

This lodge needed a makeover, and it needed it fast. More specifically, it needed new management.

"Daphne! This is a surprise."

Her father's voice was as gravelly as ever, and Daphne realized she'd lost track of time as she inspected the lobby. She'd been acting as if she were at work, not coming home.

She straightened up, nodding her thanks to Grace who stood behind Duke. Grace beamed at her, then picked up the vacuum cleaner next to the stairs and proceeded to climb up them with a determined air.

Ahh, so that was it—Grace had taken over her mom's job as head of housekeeping at the Lodge. Daphne remembered hearing somewhere—probably from her dad— that Grace's mom, Louise, had been diagnosed with MS and couldn't keep up with the workload any more.

In this small town, there weren't a lot of new job

openings, and Grace had worked on their housekeeping staff all through high school. It made sense she'd follow in her mother's footsteps.

Poor Grace. She'd had such big plans at one point. Daphne made a mental note to stop in and visit with her and Louise if she had the time. She'd only planned a quick trip, but she might be able to spare a half hour or so.

"Hi, Dad," Daphne said, going up to give her father a hug. The embrace was awkward—neither one of them had ever been the hugging type, but she had vowed to improve that. Her boyfriend, no, her fiancé, Alex always claimed that she was standoffish. She was trying to consciously change that day by day. It was hard, but she was making progress.

Her father pulled back from her, his eyebrows lowered. "What brings you back home?"

That was a tangled question. Not least because she hadn't thought of this place as home for quite some time. "Well . . ."

Perhaps it was her reluctant expression that did it, or perhaps Duke had finally become slightly empathic because he gruffly interrupted her, "Let's not stay out here in the lobby and chat. We don't have any guests scheduled to check in for the afternoon—let's talk in my rooms."

Daphne followed him behind the reception desk and into her childhood home.

It was a large suite that contained a living room, three bedrooms, and a small kitchen. When she peeked through the doorway of what used to be her old bedroom, she saw that it had been converted to an office. There was a huge desk in there, piled high with papers.

Other than the office, the rest of the place looked much as it had when she'd left, if perhaps a bit more timeworn. The couch in the living room had an indentation in the middle of it where, she knew, Duke sat every night to watch his game shows like Jeopardy and Wheel of Fortune.

When she was a kid, they'd had a competition about who could get the right answer first, and he would grunt with approval when she did. That was one of the few times he'd ever shown much interest in her brain.

All of this was after her mom had left, of course. It was sometimes hard to remember what her dad had been like before, and she sometimes wondered if she had imagined a father who once laughed as much as he frowned, who patiently taught her to ride her bike and took her out at night to tell her about the constellations in the sky. She still sometimes stopped walking to look up at night, to search out Cassiopeia and Orion and Ursa Minor. It made her feel . . . safe. Like there were things would never change, even as some things never returned to what had been.

With barely a pause in her step while the memories swamped her, she shook her head as they walked past the TV and into the kitchen. The room was painted yellow—a cheerful color she'd suggested after her mother left and her dad had sunk into a deep funk. She'd tried to brighten the place up, picking flowers to put in a vase on the kitchen table and pinning small, childish drawings to the fridge of Dad, her brother Darren, and her, all smiling and holding hands.

She remembered the first time she'd come home from

school after her mom had disappeared, to find her drawings had gone from the fridge. With a sinking feeling in her stomach, she'd peeked into the trash—and there they were, on top of the coffee grounds. She'd swallowed, her heart in her throat, and tried to hold back tears. Stubbornly, she decided that it was because she hadn't tried hard enough. Perhaps her drawings weren't good enough for her dad.

So, she tried again. She spent all afternoon drawing new pictures. She coloured neatly within the lines. She made their smiles even wider, their hands intertwined in a zigzag on the page.

The next afternoon, the fridge door was bare again, the trash bin full.

Maybe it wasn't her drawings, she tried to rationalize. He must have seen her efforts as a waste of time. He'd been busy with the Lodge before, but without her mom there, he seemed twice as busy. Twice as stressed, especially with the trouble her brother, Darren Jr., was getting into. And each night, Dad retreated further into himself. He sat on the couch starting at the TV, ignoring her and her brother.

Darren hadn't minded their father's lack of attention—he was always off with his head in the clouds. But she had cared, perhaps too deeply. With their mother gone, there was no one left in their lives who was family.

She'd thought that maybe if she made herself helpful, that would bring back her old dad. After all, he was always picking on Darren for not helping out enough around the Lodge. Maybe it would bring back the dad who wanted to show her how things worked, the one who taught her how to cook a pancake and unblock a drain.

And so, she stopped drawing and tried to do whatever else to help her dad out. She worked hard, folding towels for housekeeping, washing dishes, and eventually as a teen, cleaning rooms, serving in the dining room, and registering guests.

Eventually, her dad had come out of his shell a bit more. By then, she was on the cusp of leaving home for good, and the distance between them seemed too big to cross. It was easier to focus on her future, not her past.

It hurt her heart a little to see how much Duke was stuck in the past, preserving the way his parents had run the Lodge. Looking around his suite, it seemed like he hadn't changed anything since she left over two and a half decades ago. The only mark of the passage of time were inconsequential things, such as a box of cookies on the counter that weren't a kind they bought when she was at home.

Her mother had always insisted on home-baked cookies rather than store bought ones. "Better for you," Maxine would say. "None of that bad stuff you can't pronounce in my cookies."

Her dad went to the stove and busied himself with the kettle and teapot. With nothing better to do, Daphne sat at the table.

In silence, her father moved about the kitchen, getting down two plain mugs from the cupboard, as well as a sugar bowl and milk jug.

"Earl Grey okay?" he asked her.

She was surprised he even asked. He'd usually just made whatever he felt like, and she could either drink it or not. "Sure," she replied.

After he served the tea and they sat down across from each other, she had a hard time meeting her father's direct gaze. Instead, she glanced down into her mug and fiddled with the handle. This wouldn't be easy, but she'd made a resolution that she would do this. For herself. She deserved her moment of happiness, and this might be what it would take to get it.

However, her dad wasn't helping make this any easier for her. He sat there, drinking his tea and staring off into space. He looked a bit pale, she noticed. Was it just the short winter days with their lack of sun? It was halfway through December, and the weather had been off and on snowfalls. When it wasn't snowing, like today, it was overcast.

She'd have to just come right out with it. "Dad," she began. His gaze, which had been focused at some distant point out the window, flicked over to her. She had his attention. "There's something you should know."

He didn't bother asking, just waited, and she cleared her throat.

"Actually, two things," she amended after the silence dragged on for a heartbeat.

"First off, I want to tell you that I've been dating someone really wonderful."

Duke's eyes narrowed, and Daphne knew even before he opened his mouth that he would try to unload some of his

"Love is BS" rant on her. It was the same speech he'd given her every time she dated someone new.

She spoke quickly, before he could start. "And he's very supportive of me. In fact, he's so supportive that he encouraged me to come here to talk to you."

And he had—she wasn't stretching the truth with that statement. Alex was unlike anyone she'd ever dated before in her forty-four years. She'd given up hope that she would ever find "the one" before she met him. All the men she'd been in relationships with over the years had let her down in one way or the other.

Like Jerry in her twenties, who'd been ten years her senior, and who'd cheated on her at least ten times.

Michael, in her early thirties, had dumped her because he suddenly went from not wanting kids to wanting to start a family she had no desire for.

In her late thirties, Nathaniel had been her significant other, but he'd thought arguing was a love language, and she'd gotten tired of being shouted at.

In between had been various casual dates, often from online platforms. Some of the matches had been horribly funny, like the man who thought he would get rich quick by selling cat hair toques, and some had just been horrible, like the guy who didn't believe in soap.

She'd decided she was done with love.

But everything was about timing, wasn't it? Because that was when she'd met Alex at a work function. They hadn't worked in the same company, but they'd been seated together at a banquet table during an out-of-province hotel management conference. He was ten years younger than her, so that had been a bit of a stumbling block when they discovered they lived in the same city and he asked her out. She'd told him no, very emphatically, and suggested they become good friends instead.

She'd liked him from the first moment she met him, though. One thing eventually led to another. Before she knew it, they'd moved in together and she'd never been happier.

Never been happier, that is, until he dropped to one knee a couple of weeks ago and asked her to marry him.

Back in her dad's kitchen, she glanced down at her ring finger. She wasn't wearing the beautiful diamond ring Alex had given her because it was too loose. It was at the jewellery shop in the city, being resized.

Alex would be picking it up for her before she got back, and she couldn't wait to slip it onto her hand and show the world that she was going to be Mrs. Alex Belanger.

"I'm engaged," she blurted out now as her Dad sat there, eyebrows raised. "And, in the interest of making peace, Alex encouraged me to reach out to my family. All of them."

Duke's eyebrows began to lower, as if he anticipated what she was going to say next.

She swallowed. Her dad could still make her feel like she was that little girl who tried so hard to have her father pay attention to her, who tried so hard to make him happy to be with her.

She'd spent years trying to get him to see her as a person, to realize that she wasn't like her mom even if she looked more and more like Maxine the older she got.

Perhaps that was part of the reason her dad had had a problem with her once her mom took off? Did she remind him of what he'd lost?

Storm clouds had settled across Duke's expression. "What do you mean . . . family?"

"Exactly what I said," she told him. "I . . . I reached out to Maxine, too." It hadn't been hard to find her, and this was something that Alex had helped her with too. In fact, it had been surprisingly easy to locate her mother. She still wasn't comfortable calling someone who felt like a stranger "mom."

She hadn't found her brother, but even if she had, she wouldn't want to tell Darren Jr. her plans until right before the wedding. She would probably have to count the metaphorical silver if he came to visit any earlier, so she wasn't quite ready to find him yet.

"Dad, I would like to have both of my parents at my wedding," Daphne continued. "I'm hoping you two can bury the hatchet."

There was a long pause as she waited for his answer.

Duke threw back his head and laughed. And then kept laughing. There was an edge to his laughter, perhaps scorn or anger?

Daphne felt as if her insides were withering at her dad's response.

Duke finally managed to get himself under control as he wiped at his watering eyes and drew in a deep breath. "You've got to be kidding," he growled. "I can't believe you asked that of me. I know exactly where I'd bury that hatchet. I'll never make peace with that woman. Never."

Daphne's lips drew into a thin line. She was determined not to start an argument with her father. Her request must have come as a great shock, so she would give him time to adjust to it. She hoped he'd come around. And, if not . . . well, she would cross that bridge when she came to it.

"Okay, well . . . why don't I stay the night and we can catch up?" she changed the subject, taking a long drink from her now lukewarm tea.

His expression was suspicious, but he took her olive branch. "That would be nice," he told her. "There's a free room on the second floor you could take. Number 201."

That was the room closest to the stairs, which could sometimes be noisy for guests. They gave that room out as a last resort when they were fully booked. The rest of the time, it tended to be empty.

"Sounds good," she said. "I'll let you get back to work, then." She got up to wash out her mug. As she was doing so, she casually added, "Do you need any help around here? I'd be happy to pitch in while I'm here . . ."

But Duke shook his head, as she'd guessed he would. "Nope. Everything's under control. I have Leeroy and Grace to help me, so you can just relax and enjoy your stay."

Except she wouldn't, she knew. All she could see was how this place was falling apart, and all she wanted to do was leave as soon as she possibly could. But she pretended that everything was fine as she turned back to her father. "Thanks, Dad," she told him. "I'll do that."

They made plans to meet for dinner in the dining room at six.

2.
At the hospital

Maxine Robertson

In shock and on auto-pilot, Maxine hoisted the last heavy box of files into her SUV. Her wiry seventy-three-year-old muscles yanked at the empty uncooperative trolley and wheeled it back to the lobby of her office building. Normally, nothing could take her away from her work—her life was the IBA, Innocence Blueprint Alberta. Nothing, that is, but a middle-of-the-night emergency call from the Laurel Lake Hospital saying her dad had suffered a heart attack. She didn't remember everything the nurse had said, but her last words looped in Maxine's brain: "His prognosis is touch and go. You might want to come as soon as you can."

After the call, Maxine had raced through her condo in a state of focused panic, desperately willing her dad to hang in there. *Please don't die before I get there*, she kept repeating to herself. She threw a suitcase together, then raced to the office to gather the research files on her latest case. A nineteen-year-old had been incarcerated in 1998 for the killing of a university student. A forced confession, evidence that didn't add up, and the recent discovery that the technology used by the pseudo-experts hired by the prosecutor was a sham—all pointed to her client's innocence. This would be the fourteenth person IBA had proven to be wrongfully convicted since Maxine opened the doors in 1988.

Setting the cruise to a hundred and twenty-eight kilometres an hour, Maxine alternated between nervously tapping the steering wheel and gnawing on her fingernails. *Ah, Dad! I remember how proud you were when I went back to school to get my law degree. You always encouraged me to follow my dreams. Everyone else crucified me from the tops of their glass mountains when I left Laurel Lake.*

She looked at her hands in disgust. So much for that manicure. Was the last time she bit her nails to the quicks in a bloody but soothing release when she still lived in Laurel Lake? She thought so. She'd felt like she was in a prison of her own back then, with an uninspiring husband, a suffocating marriage, and two beautiful children that she never knew how to mother.

Maxine wasn't cut out to be a mom, had never wanted kids, but Duke had begged and begged. She'd given in, thinking maybe a child was the missing link to their disappointing marriage. Turns out what was missing from their marriage was her self-identity. She escaped all of it in 1983 to get a law degree. Her only regret was leaving Daphne and Darren without a mom. She knew what that felt like. She'd survived. She knew they could, too.

The dark greys of night were not yet losing their battle to the promise of a purply-pink and orange sunrise when Maxine pulled into the hospital parking lot. She pulled on the handle of the entrance door and rattled it. The door was locked. She pressed the buzzer, cursing all small towns for their inconveniences. In the city, she would just be able to walk in. Now, she was at the mercy of the keeper of the entranceway.

"Can I help you?"

Maxine rolled her eyes. "My dad is a patient. He had a heart attack. I was called to come as soon as I could."

"What's the name of the patient?"

Like you have so many in this ten-bed hospital that you don't know. "Robert. His name is Robert Robertson"

"And you are?"

About to lose my fucking mind if you don't open the door and let me in. "I'm Maxine Robertson, his daughter. I was called to come in right away." *What if they're stalling because he already died?*

"Yes. Robert's in the HDU—the High Dependency Unit. I'll buzz you in. Take the first two rights and you'll find him."

Maxine walked quickly to the HDU where everything slowed down. The staccato of beeps, mesmerizing bright lights, the still form of her father lying under a thin blanket, with tubes and wires connected to machines all around him, and a cannula in his nose for oxygen.

She walked in slow motion to the bed, tears flooding down her face. "Oh Dad," she whispered as she reached for his hand. She clasped it in both of hers, caressing its warmth like the rock-steady grasp he had always been for her. His veins bulged bright blue against the almost translucent, withered skin.

Maxine moved closer, laid her head near his chest, and sobbed. The steady rise and fall of his breathing comforted her. His heartbeat sounded good. It felt strong. *He can't possibly be on his way out.* Maxine drifted off for a few minutes to the gentle clicks and hums of the machines.

A nurse put a hand on Maxine's shoulder. "You must be Robert's next of kin."

Maxine wiped her eyes and nodded. "I'm his daughter, Maxine. Can you tell me what happened, please?"

"He arrived by ambulance around one in the morning in cardiac arrest. He was treated to get his heart back in regular rhythm. He responded well."

"Is he going to be okay?"

The nurse adjusted the intravenous drip. "When the doctor comes back in the morning, we'll have a better idea of what we're dealing with."

Maxine's dad had just moved into the seniors' residence a year ago. It had been the best move for him, since he was such a social guy. On their weekly phone calls, he'd said, "You can never be lonely here. Just open your door and walk down the hall." Maxine had been thankful.

"What time does the doctor usually come in?" she asked the nurse.

"Around eight o'clock and the HDU is her first stop."

"Can I stay here with him?"

"You can for the rest of tonight." She walked to the door, stopped, and turned around. "You should get a room at Laurel Lake Lodge if you're staying in town. You'll be more comfortable there and it's only five minutes up the highway. The motels are all in neighbouring towns. I imagine you don't want to drive that much."

"Right. Thanks." Maxine cringed at the thought of the Lodge, and ran her fingers over the rough bits of her chewed nail ends.

If Laurel Lake didn't come with so many bad memories, perhaps she would feel a sense of awe at the beauty of the place, like the rest of the world seemed to. But all she ever felt was disappointment and sadness, as she was overwhelmed with memories of that horrible time when the kids were little. That had been the final push to leave Duke.

"Thanks," she said watching the nurse exit the room. The Lodge had been run down when she'd left in the 1980's to get her law degree. She could only imagine how bad it was now. Duke hadn't been a genius in any part of the business. If only he'd sell the Lodge. She'd be relieved that Darren and Daphne wouldn't be strangled by that family entanglement.

She caressed her dad's pale face. Maxine's lack of mothering skills was one of only a handful of regrets she had in her life. She didn't have what it took for any kind of parenting. Her other regret was simple—moving back to Laurel Lake to marry Duke. She remembered leaving for university at seventeen and boldly announcing, "I'm never coming back to this hellhole." And yet, hypnotized with naive hopes after being sucked in by Duke's dreams, she had returned. It had taken years of misery before she mustered the courage to escape and do what she needed to do to nurture her soul and sense of purpose.

With her dad aging, Maxine had known she would need to spend some time here eventually. Up until now, she had managed with day trips to share holiday dinners with him and, occasionally, Daphne visited her in the city. Darren had left the province the second he finished school. She hadn't even had a chance to say goodbye. By the time he turned thirteen he had nothing to do with her, except to send the occasional letter every few years offering her an opportunity to invest in his latest business scam.

Every year, Maxine and her dad enjoyed a one-week cruise together. That was her birthday present to him. He always picked the destinations. Researching kept him busy and excited.

Maxine stared at her dad's flickering eyelids, willing him to open his eyes and see her. She brushed his unruly old-man eyebrows. When had those gotten so out of control? Maxine squeezed his hand. "Where do you think we should go for our cruise this year? How about Egypt? Or should we go on an Alaskan cruise again?"

Her dad's body shuddered.

Maxine stared from her dad to the machines. His heartbeat had gone up a bit, but settled down. She hoped he was just dreaming.

She clenched every muscle and began her four-by-four breathwork. Looking out the window, she whispered, "I will give anything to have more time together. Even hanging out at the Laurel Lake Lodge in a shit town that I said I would never stay another night in. I will do for you, Dad, in a heartbeat!" He was out cold, but she wondered if his subconscious heard and he was laughing in his dreams. The older she got, the more she wished she had inherited his go-with-the-flow attitude. Unlike her, nothing ever fazed him.

At seven o'clock the nurse returned to check her dad's vitals. Maxine yawned as she watched.

"You should go get some sleep," the nurse said with a gentle smile. "We're about to change shifts. Everything is looking fine here."

"Right," said Maxine. "The Lodge." She stood up and looked at her dad.

"Go sleep," said the nurse. "When you come back, he'll probably be awake and able to visit."

3.
Eve of Destruction Resources

Scout Pinson

Scout Pinson was annoyed. The rental car was not to her standards, though the rental agent claimed it was the best class of luxury car available when she'd arrived at the Calgary International Airport. The navigation system had been a pain. It didn't recognize the Laurel Lake address. The drive began to feel like a journey to the edge of the world.

"Oh, good god," Scout uttered as she walked toward the doors of Laurel Lake Lodge. Up close it looked like a teardown. The idea of sleeping there did not appeal.

From the parking lot, Scout had thought the place had a welcoming charm to it, but up close it was shabby.

Scout thought her foot was likely to go through one of the rickety wooden stairs as she stepped onto the covered porch that ran the length of the hotel.

A threadbare red carpet runner led to the entrance.

The double doors still retained the evidence of an era where quality mattered. They were solid and well-made.

Inside, she detected the sweet, musty smell of 'old building' with a top note of lemon polish and bleach.

The expansive lobby was dimly lit and deserted. No one was at the reception desk.

Scout tapped the service bell repeatedly with growing

intensity. She expected service, not time-consuming delays.

Booking the hotel had been cumbersome. It had no online presence. She'd had to make a telephone call to reserve her room. A queen size bed was the Lodge's most luxurious offering.

Behind the reception desk a door creaked open, and an older man emerged. He had a bit of egg on the corner of his mouth. Crumbs littered the front of his crumpled blue shirt.

"May I help you?" he asked, staring pointedly at her finger still poised above the bell.

"I'm Scout Pinson. I have a reservation."

"Scout, what kind of name is that for a . . . woman?" the old man muttered as he flipped through a book.

"You'd have to ask my mother. She named me," Scout said with exaggerated sweetness. She wasn't interested in gender politics with this Neanderthal.

"Hmph," was his only response.

He'd found the correct page and read carefully, his finger tracking the line as he squinted at it. "Three nights, is that correct?"

"Maybe longer if I like it. What is there to do besides stare at the lake?" she asked.

He scowled. "That's enough for most folks. Sign the register here, please."

As she did so, she noticed a name she recognized: D. DeMott. The signature was unmistakable. Why had her mother visited this out-of-the-way lodge?

The man turned to the keys mounted behind him. "This is the best guest room in the Lodge," he said, setting a brass key with a diamond shaped tag on the desk. "Room 305. It's a lake view with a balcony, ensuite and a queen-sized bed as you requested. Elevator is there," he told her, pointing to the left.

With the movement, she realized his shirt was embroidered with the Lodge's logo, and a name: Duke.

She picked up the key. "How quaint. Can someone help me get my luggage to my room, Duke? Do you have a bellhop?"

Duke shrugged. "It's not difficult to find. Exit right from the elevator, third door down the hall to your left."

Then without giving her a chance to respond, he went back through the door behind the desk.

Scout glared at the door, thinking if her look could kill, Duke would be dead, and he wouldn't even see it coming.

- - - - -

As Scout stepped out of the elevator on the third floor, she could hear a news broadcast blaring from a room to left of the elevator. The sound faded as she pulled her roller bags down the hall. Turning the key in the lock, she wondered what level of disappointment awaited her behind the door. She suspected the room would be far from her upscale standards. But when she stepped inside, she inhaled the faint whiff of lemon polish and fresh mountain air. She opened the French doors to the balcony. A gentle breeze kissed her as she breathed it in. The room was, to her surprise, quite charming, albeit dated. She might say it was reminiscent of a classic 1930s hotel in old Hollywood, not a dingy western lodge at all.

She set about hanging her clothes and making herself familiar with the electrical plug locations. There was a lack of places to plug in her computer and apparently no Wi-Fi. Her cell data was going to take a hit, but it would work providing there was cell service. A quick check verified there was service; at least something was going right.

Changing into jeans and a sweater, Scout set out to explore the Lodge. Wandering down the hall, she followed the television noise coming from down the hall.

The door to the room was ajar. As she walked past, a man was sitting in a recliner with his back to the door.

Scout had gone a few paces past the open door when a deep, male voice called out, "I was wondering when you'd show up."

Scout froze.

The man emerged from the room. There was something familiar about him. Most wanted? Famous actor, what?

"Who are you?" he asked, his deep voice bouncing off the walls.

"Sorry if I disturbed you. I just checked in and was familiarizing myself with the fire exits," she said, which was partially true. She reached out a confident hand, "Scout Pinson."

"Pleased to meet you. Pinson, any relation to Reg and Deedee Pinson?"

Who was this guy? Was he the reason her mother had come to the Lodge? "No relation," she lied.

He eyed her carefully, nodded, and turned back to his room, closing the door.

- - - - -

The entrance to the dining room was not so obvious. No signage, just an unmarked set of double glass doors, propped open. Like the lobby, it was deserted. Scout was beginning to feel creeped out by how vacant the Lodge was. At least no one was going to miss it when it succumbed to the wrecking ball.

"Hello? Can I get some service?" she called out from beside the Please Wait to the Seated sign. Her words seemed to echo into a void. "Hello?" she repeated a little louder.

The door to what she assumed was the kitchen swung open with force. A white-coated figure glared at her. "What do you want?"

"I was wondering if I could order some food?"

"We serve dinner at five." He spun on his heels as the door shut behind him.

Scout was left blinking alone in the dining room.

Turning toward the elevator while pondering whether she might have a protein bar buried in her purse, Scout nearly collided with Duke.

"My apologies," he said. "We're having some staffing issues. May I offer you toast? I can make you some back there." He waved at the reception desk.

"Oh! Yes. I'd appreciate that," she said, as her stomach rumbled. She followed him across the lobby and through the door behind the reception desk.

To her surprise, it was another world behind that door. It wasn't a staff break room, as she'd expected, but a homey living quarters. It was a little untidy, but seemed clean enough. Duke led Scout through the adequate sitting room and into a small, sunny yellow kitchen.

"Sit," he said, pulling a wooden chair away from the small table.

Taking a seat, she watched the old man fill a kettle with water, put it on to boil. With deft movements he popped two pieces of bread into the ancient-looking toaster.

"Butter and strawberry preserves okay?" he asked as he reached for a big brown teapot on a shelf. His hands shook a bit as he lowered the pot gently onto the tiled counter.

"That would be lovely. I'm sorry to be a bother." She regretted her earlier brusqueness in the face of this kindness.

"No problem. The dining room should be open, but . . ." He trailed off the thought as the toast popped up.

Duke slathered the golden bread with butter and added a dollop of preserves on the side of the plate. He set the plate in front of Scout, adding a napkin and cutlery.

"This looks perfect," she said taking a knife to spread the preserves.

The kettle whistled, he poured the water into the teapot, set it on the table, then added a small jug of milk and a sugar bowl beside it. Setting a mug for each of them on the table, Duke finally took a seat opposite her.

"Thank you so much. This is lovely, so unexpected," Scout said, after swallowing a bite of toast..

"You're our guest. I want you to be comfortable. As I

said, we've had some trouble with the dining room staff lately. Toast and tea are easy to provide." He studied her closely as she ate.

"I should have eaten something at the airport," she said, pausing to add milk and sugar to her mug, "but I just wanted to get on the road and get here. I wasn't sure how long it would take me to drive out. It is a lovely drive. It must be a bit of a challenge when it's snowing." She took another bite of toast.

"You look like her, you know," Duke said.

Scout nearly choked. "Pardon?"

"Deedee DeMott. You've got the look of her when she was younger."

"How do you know Deedee?"

"She spent a lot of time here. She was friends with my wife. They met in college. Deedee brought her artsy friends up here. We all painted together. Did she send you here to buy me out?"

"What?" she asked, taken completely by surprise. "No, she, uh, has no idea I am here. I'm here on behalf of the firm I work for."

Duke poured himself more tea. "Deedee is your mother, I presume?" Duke pressed.

"Yes. Is that a problem?"

"Not in the least. I guess you could say that I am also one of Deedee's artsy friends. There was a time I thought I was a fair-handed painter. She was here not too long ago herself. She said she needed to reset, away from everything. I gather your father travels a lot with his business? How about you? Do you live on your own?"

"I have an apartment in Vancouver. I split my time between there and Toronto. I travel a lot for work, so I am not home often. I was hoping to discuss purchasing the Lodge and land with you before I go."

He grunted noncommittally.

"Can you tell me something about the history of the Lodge?"

Duke nodded, and told her about his parents buying the land and improving the site over the years. She enjoyed his candid way of stating the facts. He explained his son showed no desire to carry on the family business.

"Don't you have a daughter?"

Duke just grunted.

A voice called from the lobby, "Duke?"

"Come in, Leeroy."

A young man in overalls came into the kitchen and looked curiously at Scout, though he didn't say anything.

Duke gave a little sigh and stood up. "I'm sure you've got things to do, Ms. Pinson. I'd best get back to work. Why don't you walk around the lake? The dining room should be open when you get back."

Scout followed him into the lobby and watched as he and the young man strolled off.

Duke's dismissal of his daughter give Scout the impression that he had little regard for a woman's ability to run a business. Perhaps women, like her mother, who gave the appearance of being dependent upon men, were more to his liking. Scout knew her mother was astute when it came to art, but she relied on her charm, rather than demonstrating her business acumen. Scout's father had always teased Deedee, calling her dangerous to the unsuspecting. Duke clearly saw Deedee differently.

- - - - -

Taking Duke's advice, Scout took a walk around the lake. It was a cool afternoon. Leaves had turned on the deciduous trees and were beginning to fall from the trees and cover the landscape. The lake was tabletop smooth. It was a very peaceful setting. A bench facing the lake invited her to sit and take it all in. Scout noted the bench had a dedication plaque.

In memory of Savario.

She knew the name. He was a visual artist. She had seen one of his paintings hanging in her mother's West Vancouver home. Was the artist perhaps one of those 'artsy friends' she'd brought here all those years ago? Was he a lover from her mother's past? Scout had a lot of questions as she gazed up at the mountains.

- - - - -

The menu in the dining room was decent enough. The pretty server with the interesting accent used her charm to effect.

Scout happily accepted her cocktail recommendation. She didn't want to go up to her empty room, so as she finished one cocktail, she ordered another.

She failed to notice other diners filing in. When her glass

was empty for the third time, she looked around for her server. That was when she noticed the old guy from the room down the hall from her was seated nearby. She also noted a young couple who were too absorbed in one another to pay her any attention.

Scout waved at the older man. He avoided eye contact with her.

That wasn't right. He should be salivating over her interest! Scout rose from her chair and stumbled over to his table.

"Good evening. Care to join me?" She put back her shoulders to elevate her chest. "I could use the company. Let me treat you."

Looking discomfited by her boldness, the man studied his hands.

"I could really use some company," she said. "Sure you can, too?"

By this time, she had attracted the attention of the young couple who exchanged looks. Scout became aware that she was making a scene. Did she seem pathetic?

"My apologies," she said, with an exaggerated bow. "I am sorry to have bothered you." She retreated to her own table.

The man followed her to her table.

"I'm sorry," he said. "Call me Eddie." He pulled out a chair and sat opposite her. "I didn't mean to offend. I'm just not used to beautiful women approaching me." He blushed a bit, to prove the point.

"Thank you," she said with a shaky smile. "I don't like

dining alone."

He smiled back at her.

"Why don't you tell me about yourself?" she said, leaning toward him.

He told her his wife had recently passed away, but that they had many happy visits to Laurel Lake, so he was here spending time remembering her.

The lovely young server returned. "Mr. Edwards, I'm so happy to see you've found a friend."

Scout ordered a glass of water and a beer for her companion. She set down her menu, "I am completely undecided. What would you recommend I try?"

The server immediately replied, "Meatloaf dinner with mashed potatoes. It's the most popular."

Eddie nodded. "I agree. It's very tasty. I'll have the same."

Scout and Eddie chatted before, during, and after the meal.

It was only when the server told them the dining room was closing that Scout realized they had been talking for several hours. She left a large tip and the two of them walked to the elevator together.

He bid her goodnight, saying he needed a walk before retiring, and went through the outside doors, leaving Scout to go up to her room alone.

It had been an interesting first day at Laurel Lake Lodge. She sat down at her laptop to write up a Letter of Intent for the purchase of Laurel Lake Lodge and its various land holdings. She considered the things she'd learned from her conversations and consulted with the maps she'd brought as she added purchase details. When the right moment came, she would give the letter to Duke and official negotiations could begin.

When she finished the paperwork, she checked the time on her phone. It was not too late to call her mother.

"Hello, darling girl," Deedee purred at the phone when she answered. "What are you up to these days?"

"Mum, why were you recently at Laurel Lake Lodge?" Scout held her breath.

"Why are you asking and how do you know that I was there? Have you been spying on me?"

"No, of course not. I saw your name on the register when I checked in."

"When you checked in?" Deedee laughed her throaty chuckle. "And why are you so deep in the mountains, my darling girl? I wouldn't think it's your sort of place at all."

"I want to buy it."

"Duke will never sell it to you."

"What makes you so sure?"

"The Lodge is Duke's legacy. He took over from his parents. He's got children to pass it to. Trust me. He will stay there forever." Deedee explained how she'd met Duke and Maxine years ago, and maintained a friendship with each of them separately after their marriage split up. "We had wonderful times there back in the old days. Me, Maxine, Savario, Roland, Ivan, Betty, Takao . . . What a crowd." She paused, lost in thought before she added, "Savario was the most talented of all. He died too young."

"I saw the bench," said Scout.

"I paid for that," Deedee said. "It was the least I could do. Laurel Lake is a magical place, darling girl. I wouldn't mess with it."

"Why? What is different about it? There are lakes all over."

Deedee was quiet for a moment before she said, "It's more than just the good memories I have. I guess it's something you should know if you're considering a purchase." She dropped her voice. "Keep this quiet. I think there's a lost Savario painting in the Lodge. If there is, it'd be worth a fortune."

"But it'd belong to Duke."

"Until we bought it from him or he gave it to me as a gift for all my years of friendship." Deedee chuckled.

We, thought Scout. *There is no 'we' in this purchase. There is only me and Eve of Destruction Resources.*

"Your father is fond of that lodge too, since it's where we met. You might break his heart if you ruined it." She chuckled again.

Scout joined the laughter. She knew her father wasn't the least bit sentimental. He was competitive, though. If he heard she was negotiating a deal, he'd send his own team to scuttle her deal, just for the pleasure of stealing her opportunity.

"Don't tell Daddy what I'm doing," Scout said.

"Scout, I stay out of your father's business, and he stays out of mine. I won't mention your business. Don't worry. But If you get the sale, I have dibs on the lost painting."

The two of them laughed

"Good luck, darling girl. Do say hello to Duke for me."

"I will. Good night, Mom."

Scout had a lot to think about when she hung up the phone.

Scout had only just been promoted to Acquisitions Lead for Eve of Destruction Resources. It was an impressive promotion, but she suspected it was less to do with her own skills and more to do with being Reg Pinson's daughter. Regardless, she was eager to prove she was up to the responsibility.

She'd gone from a junior in regional acquisitions to national in three years, and now, she was on the global team. It was the successful acquisition of oil-rich land in India, which mainly Scout had brokered when the team lead fell sick in the middle of negotiations. Sealing that deal had put her at the top of the leadership board.

A geologist report of a hole-in-the-wall place called Laurel Lake indicated it should be her next target, and here she was.

As Scout sat in her quaint room at Laurel Lake Lodge, she wondered what would happen to the people who lived here after the Lodge was gone. She shook her head to clear the thought. It wouldn't do to develop a conscience.

- - - - -

On her second day at Laurel Lake, Scout slept in. Her head ached from the drinks the night before. What had she said to her mother? Why had she called her when she was so tipsy? You never talk about a deal before it is complete.

The greater problem she had was that her memory of the conversation was a convoluted jumble of business and her mother's long friendship with Duke Laurel.

Throwing on a sweater and leggings, she quickly splashed her face with cold water and ran a brush through her hair. She needed breakfast; her stomach was growling. When she reached the dining room, the door was locked, and a hastily taped sign said they would reopen for lunch at eleven. She checked her watch. It was nine-thirty.

Duke appeared in the lobby. He was with the handsome young man he'd called Leeroy. Judging by the way Duke was pointing at the floor, they were discussing the broken tiles in the lobby.

"Good morning," Scout said with her best attempt at sounding awake and cheerful.

"Good morning," Duke said. "You're looking more relaxed today."

Leeroy was giving Scout a thorough appraisal.

Ignoring him, she focused on Duke. "Looks like I've missed breakfast. Is there somewhere nearby I can drive to grab a meal?"

"What do you want to eat?" Duke asked.

"Coffee, eggs, and toast, I guess?"

"Come on, I can feed you," he said, nodding toward his quarters. "You remember Leeroy? If you don't mind listening to shop talk, he and I can continue our discussion while I cook."

The three of them filed into Duke's kitchen. As he set about making breakfast for Scout, Leeroy and he continued their repair discussion. Scout sat silently, listening to the banter between the two men. Leeroy glanced at her periodically, blushing slightly when she caught him looking.

He was well-built, attractive. She could take that for a spin, she thought to herself, then blushed at her own inner, dirty thoughts. It had been too long since she was last with anyone. Work had really begun to get in the way of a social life. She hadn't had a steady relationship in years. Her parents had been in their late thirties when they met and married, forty when she was born. There was time.

"What brings you to Laurel Lake, Scout?" Leeroy asked, breaking her from her reverie.

"She wants to buy me out," Duke said before she could answer.

He set a plate of scrambled eggs, toast, and coffee before her, and sat at the table with his own mug of coffee.

Scout said nothing. Instead, she dug into the delicious breakfast.

"Why do you want to buy the Laurel?" Leeroy asked with a slight edge to his voice.

Again, before she could answer, Duke spoke on her behalf. "She works for a big multinational that buys up businesses and land."

Scout nearly choked on her toast.

Duke laughed. "Don't look so surprised. Did you think I hadn't figured you came with an ulterior motive? Don't worry. I'm willing to talk."

"Oh," said Scout. She was completely taken aback.

"Explain to me why your company wants to procure an

old, isolated lodge," he asked, scrutinizing her face.

"Heritage and seclusion. They'd turn it into a destination boutique hotel. Part of a tour circuit," she lied. Even as she said it, she could visualize the whole area being blown to smithereens.

Duke sighed. "Scout DeMott, you're lying to me. If you want a lie to be effective, look your victim straight in the eye," he said with an angry edge.

"It's Pinson, not DeMott. How much money would it take to make you say yes?" she asked, looking him straight in the eye.

"What's your best offer?"

"Let me get the Letter of Intent," she said.

4.

The Apprenticeship of Leeroy Lemon

Leeroy Lemon

Leeroy Lemon, age sixteen, had already spelled out "DOOK LORAL IS A . . ." on the Lodge's woodshed with the orange spray paint when he felt his left ear pinched and twisted.

"I've been thinking of repainting that wall, but orange wasn't the colour I had in mind." Duke had spoken in a calm, low voice. Leeroy was used to yelling and profanity, so he'd found Duke's voice strangely terrifying. "And if you're the best speller of the bunch, God help us."

Leeroy's other partners in crime had run off into the darkness when they saw the door of the Lodge's service entrance swing open to reveal Duke Laurel carrying a shotgun.

It wasn't loaded and hadn't been fired in his lifetime, but Leeroy didn't know that until years later.

Of the four boys in the unofficial gang, it had been decided that Leeroy would do the writing on account of him receiving a solid C- in grade nine English.

"On your feet," Duke had said, still holding him by the ear. He'd led Leeroy across the grounds toward the workshop, and as he'd stumbled and staggered over the rough ground, Leeroy's imagination conjured up all sorts of horrific scenarios awaiting him. Like spending the next few years locked in a cage in the shop, thrown scraps every few days to keep him barely alive, and being used for slave labour. Or maybe Duke would just take him out back and shoot him.

Inside the workshop, Duke had finally let go of Leeroy's ear and hit a light switch.

While Leeroy rubbed his aching ear, he'd looked about the workshop illuminated by one naked bulb dangling from the ceiling. Every nook and cranny of the workshop was crammed with spools of wire, scraps of metal, a rambling assortment of old tools hung from hooks, buckets of assorted screws and nails, and shelves holding unmarked containers.

Duke had turned sideways and reached in behind a pile of lumber and pulled out a can of paint.

"This should be enough if you don't get sloppy," Duke said, then he'd reached up to a shelf, pushed aside an old coffee urn, and taken down a paint brush.

If any guests had been awake at that late hour, they could have looked out their window across the Lodge's grounds and seen a burly man resting a shotgun on his shoulder, leading a boy built like an understuffed scarecrow carrying a bucket of paint in one hand and a large brush in the other.

When they'd arrived back at the shed, Duke tapped the writing on the wall with the barrel of the shotgun. "You know what to do," he'd said.

Leeroy had never painted anything before in his life. The

closest he'd come was the time Mrs. Willoughby hired him to paint her fence, but he'd run off with the paint and sold it to Shady the Pawnbroker who'd give you money for pretty much anything, including a set of dentures that had belonged to his mother's old boyfriend, Gordo. But this time, Leeroy would actually have to paint the wall.

"Don't just stand there," Duke had said, pacing back and forth. "The wall's not going to paint itself."

Leeroy had dipped the brush in the bucket of paint and drawn it out.

Duke had snapped, "Told you not to be sloppy. You slop paint like that and you'll run out before the job's done. That's when your real troubles begin."

Leeroy had held the brush over the bucket until the paint stopped dripping, then brought it to the wall and smeared it across "DOOK."

"It's Mister Laurel to you. Or just plain sir," Duke had said as Leeroy dipped the brush in the bucket once again.

A few more brush strokes, and the orange letters faded.

"You're going to have to do the whole wall," Duke had said. "The new paint doesn't match the old."

Leeroy dipped the brush back in the paint can, then carefully brought it to the wall. He was almost getting the hang of this.

"Keep the brushing moving the same direction. And don't stop until the whole wall's covered." Duke started walking toward the Lodge. "And don't you go running off. You don't want to have to ask your delinquent friends to pick buckshot out of your butt."

Leeroy remembered glancing over his shoulder as Duke disappeared into the Lodge. He'd known he was fast enough to make it to the cover of the trees by the lake. He could take his chances with buckshot in his butt. But he didn't. He kept painting, the fresh white paint transforming a wall that had been dull, grey, and faded.

A few minutes later, the service entrance screen door had banged open, and out stepped Duke, no longer carrying the shotgun. Instead, he had a plate of sandwiches in one hand and a blanket under the other arm. Without a word, Duke had held the plate out to the boy. Leeroy stared back, not knowing what to do.

"If you don't eat these sandwiches, I will," Duke said. The boy tentatively took the plate, then devoured the sandwiches.

"Looks like you were never taught to chew your food," Duke said, walking back and forth, closely examining the fresh paint on the old woodshed's wall. "Well, I've seen worse paint jobs in my life. But you can't just paint the one wall. Seems to me you're going to have to paint the whole shed, the way it's looking. You can finish the job tomorrow morning."

Duke took the empty plate from Leeroy and started walking back toward the workshop. Leeroy followed, bringing the brush and paint can.

Inside the workshop, Duke had pointed to a shelf and said, "Clean the brush with turpentine. Third bottle on the left marked, 'CHAIN LUBE'." He walked over to a steep stairway that led to an opening in the ceiling. Setting the blanket at the bottom of the stairs, he said, "When you're done, there's a cot up by the window. You can stay if you want. Daisy takes care of the mice. Breakfast's at six."

Leeroy felt a huge wave of relief wash over him. Tonight, he wouldn't have to sleep under the bridge by Candle Creek, or in Morgan's old shed where the rats ran over him at night. And he wouldn't have to steal a bag of chips from 7-Eleven for breakfast.

It had been this way for two months, since he'd been kicked out of the trailer to make room for his latest baby half-sister. His mother's latest boyfriend was long gone, and she'd never been able to hold a job for more than a few weeks. She'd been a server at the Roadkill Cafe, did cleanup on weekends at the mill, worked as a flagger when they paved the road out to Laurel Lake, and most recently was a housekeeper at Laurel Lodge, though she'd been fired last week. Leeroy was told to move out of the trailer the day after his sixteenth birthday, which was also the last day he'd bothered going to Twin Creeks High.

As Duke turned to leave the workshop, Leeroy had found his voice, and said, "Mr. Laurel . . . thanks . . . sir."

Duke hesitated, then walked on, raising his arm in a dismissive wave.

- - - - -

The next morning, and every morning for the next fourteen years, Leeroy knocked on the service entrance of the Lodge at 6:00 a.m. The door swung open, and Leeroy stepped into the warm kitchen where Duke was already at the table, staring down at an old envelope on the wobbly wooden table. A carpenter's pencil in hand, he'd be writing his list for the day.

"Good morning Mr. Laurel, sir," Leeroy always said, and Duke never lifted his eyes from the list. He just grunted, and grumbled, "What's so good about it?" When he was done scratching with the pencil, he'd slide the list over to Leeroy and say, "Nothing here we can't handle."

Duke's handwriting was a challenge to read, but over the years, Leeroy had learned Duke's shorthand.

"UPS 6" was "Unplug the sink in room 6." If more than a plunger was likely needed, he'd write it, "UPS 6+."

"LB 12." Light bulb out in Room 12.

Then, there was the dreaded "3RK." Three rats spotted in the kitchen. Occasionally, there was "SLOT," which was "Shitload of Trouble" for any new problem that didn't have a code. On bad days, the list carried onto both sides of the envelope, and as the years went by, there were two or three envelope days.

Leeroy would look the list over and slowly nod, pass it back across the table, then scarf down his bacon and eggs while Duke drank his coffee in gloomy silence.

Duke would fold the list and stuff it in the chest pocket of his coveralls. He'd push back his chair with the back of his legs as he stood, then silently trudged off to the workshop. Leeroy would follow behind, keeping a respectful few paces back, as Duke crossed the grounds.

The workshop contained pretty much everything they'd need for most of the jobs on the list.

"There's nothing we can't handle. If you can't fix what

needs fixing with what's in the shop, it means you're lacking ingenuity," Duke would often say. His inventory of essential supplies included: a staple gun, bailing twine, nails and screws of assorted sizes, duct tape, electrical tape, rodent traps, silicone, superglue, tar, tarps, and weed killer. His basic go-to tools included a hammer, staple gun, air compressor, axe, sledgehammer, power drill, circular saw, handsaw, screwdrivers, and a collection of crescent wrenches. Of course, he also had paint, including a number of tins that were leftovers from when Greyhound repainted the bus depot a few years back.

Duke's approach to lodge maintenance was a process of crisis management, solving problems as they came up instead of wasting his energies on the prevention of hypothetical problems. And from his father, Robert, he'd learned the importance of self-reliance.

With the completion of a repair job, he'd often say, "I told you there's nothing we can't handle. Why pay some so-called expert when you can damn well do it yourself?"

Other times, Duke would proudly state, "I've kept this place together with enough duct tape to reach the moon and back, but that's what gives the place its character. And people want character."

When one of the staff suggested Duke fix the squeaky stairs, he raised his chin and said, "My father told me, when I took over this place, remember one thing! Restaurants don't sell steak. They sell the sizzle. And these stairs are our sizzle!"

Duke would stand at the door of the workshop, squint at

the list on the envelope, then mumble something like, "Electrical tape, two rolls. Plunger—the black one—and a bottle of bleach." With each item named, Leeroy would scamper around the old workshop, track down the needed item, and toss it in the wheelbarrow. "Bottle of superglue . . . better make it two. Sledgehammer. Drill and three-quarter-inch bit. Twelve two-inch screws. Nine-volt battery."

When Duke reached the end of the list, Leeroy would push the wheelbarrow full of supplies back up the hill toward the Lodge, and Duke would say, "Job one. Room 203. Plunger and bleach."

Through the course of the day, they would move from job to job, Duke completing the repair while Leeroy passed supplies as needed and occasionally held something in place when Duke ran out of hands.

Three years to the day Leeroy began working at the Lodge, Duke handed him a screwdriver and said, "I need all the screws on these hinges as tight as you can get them. Got it?"

Leeroy nodded in disbelief. Duke Laurel was trusting him to screw on a door hinge. Leeroy had watched Duke replace the hinges on countless doors, but could he meet his high standards? Duke disappeared for a while to attend to an irate guest in the dining room and Leeroy began, his fingers trembling, and with each screw, he turned that screwdriver with every fibre of the muscles in his scrawny arms. Just as he was tightening the last screw, Duke came down the hall, grumbling, "What's the world coming to? Complaining about a false eyelash floating in his soup . . .

It's not like it's going to kill him . . . I could show him something really worth complaining about!"

Duke snatched the screwdriver out of Leeroy's hand and meticulously inserted it in each and every screw and tried to give it a twist. With the final screw, Duke handed the screwdriver back to Leeroy and said, "I've seen worse door hinge jobs in my life."

From that day, ever so gradually, Duke allowed Leeroy to take on more repairs under his watchful eye.

- - - - -

The next turning point in Leeroy's unofficial apprenticeship came after the fourth time in four months, the septic system backed up, made apparent by a brown sludge emerging from all of the drains on the bottom floor of the Lodge.

As the pumper truck drove off for the fourth time, Duke shook his head and said, "Every time I have to call out that damn honey wagon, it costs me three hundred bucks."

For the first time, Leeroy saw the usually cocky, confident Duke didn't have an answer to this current dilemma. It was the first time Duke hadn't said with confidence, "It's nothing we can't handle." Instead, he looked off into the distance as if he was lost, and said in a low voice, "A new septic system . . . well, that would pretty much bankrupt me."

"What about the lake?" Leeroy said. Duke's head snapped back as if he'd been bopped on the nose. "It's probably a bad idea, but the lake's pretty big and the Lodge's pretty small."

Duke turned to look out at the lake that was a mere hundred metres from the Lodge. He started to rub his bristly chin between his thumb and index finger. Leeroy sensed that Duke hadn't immediately dismissed his idea. After a long silence, Duke said, "I've heard of worse ideas."

At the end of October, when the Lodge was empty of guests, Duke borrowed a backhoe from a neighbour who owed him a favour. Early the next morning, a flatbed truck delivered a pile of pipes that were dumped behind the shop and covered with tarps. As soon as the sun went down that evening, Duke and Leeroy got to work.

The next morning, after they'd covered all evidence of their digging with boughs from the forest, an exhausted Leeroy dragged himself back toward the shop. "Hey!" Duke called in a tired voice. Leeroy stopped and turned. "I've seen worse . . ." Then, Duke paused, waved his hand dismissively, and trudged off toward the Lodge.

Leeroy collapsed onto his cot in the workshop. Exhausted from a long night of hard, nasty, dirty work, they'd done it, and Duke was pleased.

It didn't get any better than this.

5.
Now this changes everything

Daphne

Daphne grabbed the key from behind the counter for room 201. She marked her stay off in the Lodge ledger: one night, checking out the next day, room fee complimentary.

She went back to her car to grab her overnight bag and then she spent the rest of the afternoon in 201 on her laptop, answering emails. Technically she'd taken a couple days off from her job, but there were fires that only she could put out, even from far away. Once she was done, she glanced at her phone—it was just past six o'clock. She hurriedly splashed some water on her face and ran a brush through her hair. She made her way back downstairs again.

From the dining room came the clink of cutlery and the muted tone of lodge guests. She walked in and glanced around from beside the 'Please Wait to be Seated' sign. There was a tall and lanky bearded man picking at the plate of food in front of him. He was sitting alone. The server came up to him and Daphne heard her ask if she could get him anything else, but he just shook his head.

The young woman caught sight of Daphne and hurried over. "Can I help you?"

Daphne smiled at her. The young woman had a heavy accent—Italian, she guessed. "I'm just here to have dinner with my father. Is Duke here yet?"

The question was a bit rhetorical, since it was pretty clear he wasn't sitting at any of the tables. However, Daphne reasoned that he could be in the kitchen behind the swinging doors. He often liked to personally oversee all aspects of the Lodge.

The young woman's eyes widened and she exclaimed, "Oh! You are Duke's daughter?" Then she smiled and stuck out her hand.

Daphne shook it, slightly bemused at the awed expression on the young woman's face.

"Pleased to meet you. My name is Celina. I am here visiting your country for right now. Work exchange program."

Daphne wondered if the girl thought that she would now be her boss in addition to her dad. "That's longer than I'll be staying," Daphne assured her. "I'm just here for the night visiting."

"Oh," Celina exhaled and seemed immediately more relaxed, so Daphne felt she'd guessed correctly.

"You are welcome to take a table and wait." Celina gestured around the dining room.

Daphne glanced around. "Tell you what," she said. "Why don't I run and get my dad, then I'll be back?"

"Yes," Celina said. "If I am not here when you return, sit down wherever you would like."

"Thank you."

Daphne stepped behind the reception desk and knocked on the door that led to her dad's apartment.

There was no answer.

She knocked again, more loudly in case he was in the bathroom, but she still heard no response.

"That's strange," she said. She tried the knob. The door was unlocked. That was perhaps not so unusual, considering he was probably in and out of his place all day, but it made her pause. She felt a pang of worry stab her stomach.

She opened the door. The lights were almost all out, but there was a soft glow coming from the half-closed door of her old bedroom. The space that was now Duke's office.

Her dad must have turned on the desk lamp there.

"Dad?" she called out tentatively, taking a step forward.

No answer. But now that she was in the suite, she thought she could hear something. It sounded a bit like a moan, a bit like heavy breathing. Maybe it was just her imagination, but shivers raced up and down her spine. "Dad?" she called again, taking another step inside the dark living room.

This time, she was sure of it: a moan, coming from the only room with a light on. She fumbled against the wall for the living room light switch, and blinked when the room was flooded with brightness. The sitting room was empty, but the dim office light beckoned her forward.

When she got there, she was a bit surprised to find the room empty. The desk faced the door, stuck in the middle of the room at an angle, and bookcases lined the walls. It was a large, old wooden desk, and she wondered how her dad had even got it in the room. It was huge.

The hairs on her neck stood up when she heard another moan, louder this time. She pushed the light switch on the wall. Now, she could see what she'd missed in the dim light: the office chair wasn't where it should be. She stepped closer and saw a pair of legs poking out from behind the desk.

"Dad!" she exclaimed, hurrying around the desk. He was lying on the floor, face down. For a moment, her heart stopped—was he still alive? But then she bent over him and heard a moan issue from him again. "Dad, can you hear me?"

He didn't seem able to answer. She fumbled out her phone and pressed in 9-1-1. As the operator's voice came on the line, she shouted out, "My dad's had a bad fall! Please help. Help me!"

6.

This is worse

Leeroy

Over the years, Leeroy had absorbed Duke's idiosyncratic methods of plumbing, electrical, and carpentry. Leeroy knew he was learning from a master. After he completed a job, Duke would inspect Leeroy's work. He'd often find something that could be improved—a bit more tape here, a little less sloppy on the glue there. But occasionally, Duke would say, "I've seen worse jobs," and Leeroy felt a flush of pride.

For fourteen years, Leeroy slept in that loft in the workshop, and every morning, he'd sit down to breakfast while Duke would scribble out his list of jobs for that day. Leeroy would also get lunch and dinner, and every Saturday, he'd find an envelope with some cash under his plate at dinner.

But this morning, Leeroy pushed the door open to the kitchen, and Duke's chair at the table was empty.

It was the day after Duke Laurel's stroke, and though Leeroy tried to eat breakfast as he always did, that empty chair across the table, Duke's chair, made him bolt down his breakfast and leave as quickly as he could.

He spent the rest of the day wandering aimlessly around the Lodge grounds or sitting for hours in the forest by the lake under a tree—the same tree he'd escape to as a kid when things got crazy at home. Without Duke there to tell him what to do, the firm ground Leeroy had tread upon for half his life had suddenly crumbled away.

The second morning, he pushed through the service entrance, walked into the kitchen for breakfast, then stopped. A woman was working on a laptop at the breakfast table. She was sitting in Duke's place.

The woman looked up, and Leeroy's eyes immediately went to his boot tops. He bent down to tighten up a lace, and when he was just about to tighten the other, the woman said, "Hi, Leeroy."

Leeroy stood, raised his head, and took a deep breath. "That's Mr. Laurel's spot."

The woman sighed heavily, then rose from her chair, crossed the room, and held out her hand. "Don't you recognize me? I'm Daphne. Duke's daughter." After an awkward pause, Leeroy gave her a limp handshake then dropped his hand and held it behind his back.

So, this was Daphne the adult version. She'd been a few years ahead of him in school, but he didn't remember much about her. He did remember that she dated Jared Nelson, the guy who masterminded the spray painting raid on the Lodge back when Leeroy was in school. It had taken Leeroy twenty-five years to realize that raid had everything to do with Duke telling Jared to stay away from his daughter. But that was ancient history, and now Jared ran a successful construction company specializing in decks and railings, while Daphne had just been a collection of vague memories and rumours. Until now.

Duke never talked about her, so the image of Daphne that had formed in Leeroy's mind came from what he'd heard through the Lodge staff rumour mill. She'd lived on the streets of East Van, been a Vegas showgirl, a contortionist for the Cirque de Soleil, a backup singer for Leonard Cohen, and served time for embezzlement. To ask Duke about these rumours—well, that was out of the question.

But this morning, here was Daphne in the flesh, sitting in Duke's chair at Duke's kitchen table, working on a laptop computer, a device Duke would have choice names for that Leeroy preferred not to think about in the presence of a lady.

Daphne didn't look nearly as scary as Leeroy had imagined, but Duke taught him to never be fooled by outward appearances. Maybe she had a friendly smile, but Leeroy knew it took more than a smile to run a place like Laurel Lake Lodge. The few times that Duke mentioned her, Leeroy was left with the impression that Daphne wasn't cut out for working at the Lodge. But here she was, looking like she was trying to run the place.

"I understand you were my father's right hand," Daphne said.

Leeroy shrugged and said, "Well . . . I guess. Something like that." He bent down once again and pulled up his right sock, then his left.

"A guest is having trouble opening the French doors in Room 305. I tried, but they just wouldn't budge. I'd really appreciate it if you'd head up there and take a look."

Obviously, this woman didn't know how things were done around here. First breakfast, then the job list for the day, then gather the supplies, then . . .

"Duke, I mean, Mr. Laurel always opened stuck doors," Leeroy said, looking up at Duke's favourite painting, an image of the Lodge as it appeared from the top of the mountain. "He's the only one who knew how. I'm not sure if it's something I can handle."

Daphne sighed deeply once again. She gave Leeroy a look he'd seen before, like when his mother was desperate for him to bring in some firewood or shovel the driveway so she could drive to work. He knew it was the look of desperation.

Leeroy turned, pushed his way out through the service entrance door, and headed for the workshop. Duke had this magic touch with the doors at the Lodge. Leeroy had watched him open jammed doors countless times as his assistant, but now it was up to him.

A few minutes later, he was heading up the stairs with the tools Duke used for the job. Daphne stood in the lobby and looked at Leeroy with alarm. "You're going to use a hammer and crowbar to open the French doors?"

"That's how it's done around here," Leeroy said.

- - - - -

Leeroy knocked on the door to Room 305. It swung open abruptly, and there stood Scout Pinson in a cream coloured linen pant suit, navy blue jacket, and leather dress boots, waving an unlit cigarette and motioning toward the French doors.

"What's the point of a balcony if the damn doors don't open? Or should I just smoke in the room? What kind of hotel is this?"

"Um, yeah, the doors stick once in a while," Leeroy said, ignoring her cigarette in a non-smoking room. He fixed his eyes on the French doors as he crossed the room, clutching the hammer in one hand and crowbar in the other. "Mr. Laurel always said that's part of the charm of the place."

"Charm? You call doors that won't open part of the charm?"

Leeroy's hands trembled as he checked the door handle, got down on his knees, wedged the crowbar tentatively in place between the two doors, and gave it a few taps with the hammer. He nudged the doors with his hand, but they didn't move. Leeroy fumbled the hammer and tried to hold the crowbar steady as he made a second attempt. Still, the doors wouldn't budge. After three more unsuccessful attempts, there were beads of sweat on his forehead, and his breathing getting heavier.

"What's the problem?" Scout said, fidgeting with the cigarette in one hand and poised with a lighter in the other. "Does it usually take this long?"

"Well, not usually. But Mr. Laurel . . . he's always done it before. I've seen him do it a million times." He tapped the door again and gave it a nudge. Still nothing. "Don't smoke in here. You'll get a huge cleaning fee."

Scout scowled, but Leeroy turned back to the door.

Leeroy's frustration was magnified by his feeling of embarrassment. "I'm sorry it's taking so long. It's just that . . . it's just that . . . usually there are two of us, and . . ."

Scout set her cigarette and lighter down on a table and

said, "Could I give you a hand?"

Leeroy paused and looked up at Scout. Her voice had lost its angry edge. "Well . . . I'm not sure if . . ."

"Just tell me what to do. Between you and me, we'll get these damn doors open. Unless you don't think I'm capable," she said, stepping toward him, crossing her arms and narrowing her eyes.

"Well, it's just that usually I'm on the other side of the doors," Leeroy said.

"You mean, out on the balcony?" Scout said, tilting her head.

"Yeah. But I wouldn't expect you to . . ."

"I don't get it. How do you get out on the balcony if the doors are stuck?"

Leeroy slowly raised his arm and pointed toward the end of the room.

"Through the window?"

"Yes. And then I crawl along that part of the roof to get to the balcony."

"You're kidding." Scout walked over to the window and looked out onto the narrow section of roof leading to the balcony. "Well," she said in a matter-of-fact voice, "if that's what it takes to open the doors, I guess I'm heading out the window."

"Oh, no," Leeroy began. "I don't think that's a good . . ."

"Listen. Leeroy, is it? If it takes two people to get this window open, and we're the only two people currently in this room, I don't see any alternative." She headed for the closet, threw on a fur-trimmed leather jacket, then strode across the room to the window.

Scout pulled the window open, and was met with a blast of cold air.

"You're sure you want to do this?" Leeroy said. "I mean, it's not normal for guests to . . ."

"I'm not a normal guest, Leeroy." Scout slung a leg over the windowsill and climbed out on the flat roof. Motionless, on all fours, she gasped, "Oh, my god!"

"You really don't have to . . ." Leeroy called out the window.

"I'm fine! I think I'm fine! Yes, I'm definitely fine!" Scout began a slow, deliberate crawl across the roof. She finally reached the balcony, then awkwardly slid on her stomach over the railing and tumbled into the safety of the balcony.

Struggling to her feet, she surveyed the balcony and said, "Are you sure these railings are to code?"

"Am I what?" Leeroy shouted from the other side of the glass of the doors.

"I said, are you sure these railings are to code?"

"Ah, I think so? Yeah? No? Um . . . the railings," Leeroy called back. "Mr. Laurel said they were to code when the Lodge was built, but people are a lot taller than they used to be, so now they seem low."

"Interesting logic," she said with a shiver. "Okay, Leeroy. Let's get a move on. It's freezing out here. Tell me what to do."

"Reach up to where the wooden frame meets the glass. Push up on the wooden edge as hard as you can."

Scout reached up and pressed the heel of each hand

against the molding. "I should have worn my gloves!" she shouted.

"What was that?" Leeroy called back.

"Nothing! Just get to work before my fingers start to drop off!"

Leeroy nodded, then dropped back down to his knees, wedged the crowbar in place, and gave it some taps with the hammer.

"Got it?" Scout called.

Leeroy gave the doors a nudge with his shoulder, then shook his head. He gave the crowbar a few more taps with the hammer, then another shove with his shoulder. Still, the doors wouldn't budge.

"Maybe you need to . . ." Scout began, but Leeroy watched in horror as a large chunk of snow fell from the roof above and broke on the railing behind Scout's head, exploding into a shower of snow. This was followed by her blood-curdling shriek.

"You okay?" Leeroy yelled.

"Is getting buried by an avalanche part of the process of opening this damn door?" Scout said, frantically brushing the snow out of her hair.

Leeroy figured that was it. Scout would be done helping. But then, to his amazement, she lifted her trembling arms and pushed upward on the door.

Before he dropped to his knees for his next try, Leeroy couldn't help but notice Scout's lips. They were purple. He knew there was no time to waste. He needed to get more aggressive.

Duke always told Leeroy opening these doors was a delicate job that required patience. But Duke never had a freezing lodge guest out on the balcony. This present situation called for drastic action. Leeroy swung that hammer aggressively, then gave the doors a nudge with his shoulder.

"You're close!" Scout shouted, still pushing up on the door. "Give it all you've got!"

Leeroy took a deep breath, stepped back, then threw himself against the French doors. When his shoulder met the doors, he felt them swing open. Yes! He'd done it! Duke would be so proud!

But his celebration was short-lived. The force of the opening doors had knocked Scout across the balcony. Leeroy dropped the crowbar and hammer, and lunged forward as Scout hit the balcony's low railing. As she tumbled backwards, Leeroy managed to grab the pair of fashionable leather boots just before they disappeared over the edge.

"I've got you!" Leeroy shouted. "At least, I'm pretty sure I've got you!" He was immediately worried that while he held Scout's boots, the rest of her would slide out and free-fall to the ground below. But for now, Scout was still in her boots, and flailing her arms. Leeroy let go with his left hand and grabbed her wrist. In one very inelegant motion, Leeroy hauled Scout up and over the railing.

Scout's eyes were like saucers, her mouth hanging open. Leeroy helped her to her feet, then held her arm to guide her back through the open doors and into the room.

Strangely, through all of this—falling backwards over the

railing, nearly plunging to her death, then being perilously rescued by Leeroy—Scout didn't let out a peep through those purple lips of hers. No screams, shouts, or screams of profanity. Nothing. Leeroy concluded that she was just too cold to make a sound.

He lowered Scout into a chair, then pulled a quilt off the bed and wrapped it around her.

"I really appreciate your help. I mean, I've seen worse . . . I mean, you did great," he said. "Just hold on a second. I'll be back."

Leeroy bolted from the room, down the stairs, through the lobby, and into the bar. He grabbed a bottle of brandy and headed back into the hall. As he was passing the open office door, he heard Daphne's voice.

"Leeroy! Have you got a second? I want to introduce you to our new employee." She indicated behind herself to an earnest looking young man gripping a folio of papers, who was staring back at Leeroy.

Leeroy waved dismissively, "Can't right now."

Daphne scowled. She stepped forward and hissed, "I was just informed by a guest looking from the parking lot that he doesn't believe our balcony railings are up to code. Do you think that's possible?"

Leeroy was in a rush to get back to Scout, but he paused and said, "It's not the railings that are the problem. People are taller than they used to be. But don't worry about it. We can fix the railings. I know a guy who can help us with it. You might know him, too. Anyway, it's nothing we can't handle."

Daphne gave him a puzzled look. "That's reassuring . . . but what are you doing with that bottle of brandy?"

"Just finishing off repairs to those French doors in Room 305," he said, and he ran up the stairs before Daphne could say another word.

7.
The broth is spoiled

Leo Bouchard

The breeze on the third-floor balcony of room 304 was cool but inviting. Closing his eyes, Leo Bouchard imagined the drop. It would take very little to go over the side and end his life.

Should his death be ruled a suicide, it would haunt Ana, even though they had broken up. He didn't want her to blame herself, so he was determined to make his death seem accidental.

He jostled the rickety railing. The displaced snow fell in a clump to the ground. He imagined his body sprawled out below, and a torrent of nausea hit him. He'd cause psychological trauma to whoever found him. He didn't want that, either.

A noise in the distance caused him to turn. He had to shield his face from the orange glow of the setting sun to see.

Near the lake, a woman paced. She held her phone to her ear and gestured wildly in what could only be a very intense conversation. He recognized her as Daphne, the distracted woman who'd checked him into his room with what she said was a new computer system.

On the day he'd arrived, it seemed like she had a lot on

her mind, but he had also noticed the firm set of her jaw and the dark circles under her eyes. Should his death be blamed on negligence by the Lodge, it'd surely be closed down. From what he could see, it looked like the place was barely holding on.

Leo dragged his hands over his face with a sigh, and shut the balcony door behind him. He cringed at the crack as it slammed shut.

It was neither fate that had brought him to Laurel Lake Lodge, nor a deep desire to stay in the wilderness. An internet search had revealed that the Lodge was small, old, and relatively far from the area's main attractions.

Leo did not want someone he knew to find his body after his death. He imagined a faceless stranger discovering it instead. During the hours he'd spent on the balcony, he had witnessed guests exploring the area, glimpsed into the lives of the staff, and, on one particularly snowy day, saw a child laughing while hopping into the footprints left by their father's boots. It seemed every day more difficult to follow through with his plan to end his life. At least, he thought, Christmas had come and gone, and he had successfully missed a family holiday.

Leo's parents, along with his younger brother, were lawyers. Their grit and ability to manipulate facts and remain composed left Leo feeling uncomfortable and idiotic. Their charisma and charm dumbfounded him, and he chastised himself yet again for his reserved nature. His height only added to his image of himself as a blundering giant, making it nearly impossible for him to blend in. There were very few people with whom Leo felt comfortable. Conversing with most people brought on immense feelings of apprehension and embarrassment.

Anastasia had been his vivacity. Her push was the reason he had entered the culinary arts program. They had been twenty and in love, lying in bed lazily and whispering their secret dreams. He remembered how the sun pouring through the window had made her skin glow and her hazel eyes look like a forest. She'd listened to his grumblings about his current classes and his dream of being a chef. It had immediately sent her on a mission to help his dream come true.

It was only with Anastasia by his side that he had overcome his terror and told his parents he was changing his study program. Insults followed the statement, while Anastasia's grip on his hand became increasingly tighter. After a minute of their ranting, Anastasia snapped. She yelled over them to get them to stop. The following ten years seemed all too short, but it was full of memories that crept into his mind constantly.

The shift had happened slowly. In the beginning, Anastasia would lightheartedly urge Leo to take action. She pushed him to make changes and take risks. She complained gently when it was warranted.

These gentle encouragements had transformed over time. In the beginning Anastasia's faith in him urged him to take meaningful steps to improve his positions. Then she began to beg him to take care of his mental health, to quit toxic jobs, and to explore what gave him joy. These suggestions were made seriously and frequently, then more often with frustration and finally with anger at his inability to do anything to improve his life without pressure from her.

He knew she was irritated that his anxiety stalled him. He understood that she was annoyed when he convinced himself that he would get around to doing something later. Finally, his inaction, despite his obvious unhappiness, led her to give up saying anything at all.

Leo tried to scrape the memory of her leaving him out of his mind, but that scene lived in his head with far too much clarity.

Tears had been streaming down her face when she'd shouted, "You're paused, Leo. You're just letting this miserable existence happen to you! You don't have to listen to every suggestion I make, but dear lord, do something. I need to grow, Leo, and I can't with you. I can't stay stuck, begging you to do better for yourself while you drop lower into a pit." She'd shaken her head at the door and told him, "I have to save myself."

The door shut behind her and the only sound in the apartment was the thump of his heart against his ribcage.

In his imagination he replayed what would have happened if he'd run after her and changed her mind. But he hadn't run.

He hadn't done anything but listen to the thud of his heart, shocked it was still beating when his world had ended.

8.
Opportunity knocking

Darren Laurel Jr.
(who prefers to be known as Clint)

Driving into the town of Laurel Lake was surreal. This place had always represented failure to Darren. But today, with the sun glinting off the snow on the mountain peaks, he could finally envision something different here.

- - - - -

Darren Laurel Jr. had been tired of being himself. Darren could never quite find the success he'd felt he was destined to have. He decided the problem was his name. How could someone called Darren succeed? Darren was the wimpy dad on *Bewitched*. He wanted to be Clint Eastwood. No one messed with Clint. And so, he started introducing himself as Clint Savage.

Clint Savage knew this was a rare business opportunity. It was the closest thing you could get to printing money. And it was even legal. Everyone knew there were huge profits to be had in nursing homes, and here was his chance to get in on this lucrative industry. All he needed was a couple million to join the investment group that would build the Fountain of Youth Retirement Resort in Abbotsford. Like every venture he'd undertaken before, Clint Savage approached this one with contagious gusto and bulletproof confidence.

Ten years ago, he'd said with chest-thumping bravado, "Who wouldn't want to have a robot clean their gutters?" Three years later, it was, "Crickets will revolutionize the North American diet!" And just two years after that he knew, "Glamping in Florida is the greatest untapped tourism market in the world!"

Unfortunately, it turned out that gutter-cleaning robots were only good for creating a litany of lawsuits, McDonald's wasn't interested in cricket-burgers, and folks thought camping with alligators during a hurricane lacked a certain charm. Those were problems for a Darren.

For Clint, things were different. Zero chance of failure. But there was a hitch.

Unlike his last three major ventures, Clint couldn't rely upon his in-laws as a source of funding. He'd burned through three marriages into well-heeled families, but there was no fourth on the horizon.

Forced to seek out other sources of cash, he began knocking on doors, and in each case, the door was resoundingly slammed in his face. Adding to his desperation were the demands of the rent on his luxury condo in Vancouver's West End, the lease on his Audi Quattro coupe, and the day-to-day expenses of moving within his high-flying social circle. He was balancing precariously upon the edge of a financial precipice.

His last desperate attempt to round up outside investment was a pitch to an old St. Swithen's Collegiate schoolmate, Richard "Winky" Smyth-Washburn. He was with a company, Eve of Destruction Resources, which wasn't exactly in the nursing home business, so this was a Hail Mary pitch.

"I like your idea in principle, Darren, but that's not usually our area. We're into resource development," Smyth-Washburn said over a lunch at Le Crocodile. "But here's what I'll do for you. I'll run the idea past Scout."

"Scout?" Cint said.

"Yeah. My boss, so to speak."

"How about lining up a meeting with the three of us?"

"That's a possibility. Problem is, Scout's been off somewhere in the mountains trying to buy out some geezer. His sad little lodge is getting in the way of one of our developments. Scout figures it'll be easy pickings."

Clint quickly leaned forward to rest his hands on the edge of the table and said, "What's the name of this sad little lodge?"

"Jeez, I don't know. Why the interest?"

"Just curious, that's all," Clint said, failing at his attempt to sound nonchalant. "Can you find out for me?"

"Of course," Smyth-Washburn said with a shrug of his shoulders. He pulled out his phone and fired off a text. A moment later it binged.

Smyth-Washburn looked at the screen, "Here we go. It's called Laurel Lake Lodge, and it's a hundred and ten kilometres . . ."

Clint jumped up out of his chair and said, "Thanks for the lunch, Winky. We'll be in touch."

Smyth-Washburn gave Clint a puzzled look. "Where are you going, Darren? We haven't even ordered!"

"Call it a family emergency. Gotta run! And it's not Darren. It's Clint. Clint Savage."

"And no one ever calls me Winky," Smyth-Washburn said, shaking his head.

- - - - -

Darren took a deep breath as he turned into the driveway to the Laurel Lake Lodge. The building loomed ahead of him, and for the first time, Darren saw that it represented opportunity. He parked his car and looked around. Yes. There was definitely opportunity for him here after all.

9.

The music in the art

Alistar Montgomery

Alistar Montgomery stood in the entrance to the Lodge. His blond hair reached his mid-back and flowed freely. He wore a multicoloured shirt and loose-fitting pants. He had prominent cheekbones and his steel blue eyes twinkled amid laugh lines. He held an awkwardly large cello case, covered with dents and scratches that attested it was as well-travelled as he was.

A child ran by and just missed hitting his head on Alistar's cello case.

"Excuse me, I am so sorry." A man dressed in a hoodie and sweatpants shuffled by in chase of his child with a frantic look, maybe hoping to protect his mouthful of teeth. Alistar acknowledged the man with a nod and a "hang loose" hand motion. Alistar scooped his cello up against his body and walked to the front desk.

"Good afternoon, sir. Welcome to Laurel Lake Lodge. I'm Daphne. Are you checking in?" She smiled up from her keyboard.

"Hey, Daphne, a pleasure to meet you," Alistar replied. "Single room under Alistar Montgomery."

She nodded as she looked back down at her computer screen. Her keyboard clacked as she entered his name. The sound reminded Alistar of a series of notes that had not found their sequence in his Staves notebook yet. Alistar watched the back of his eyelids, imagining his fingertips gently hugging the strings as they moved along the frets. He furrowed his brow as an off-pitch note rang clear in his mind.

"Here is your room key, Alistar. You are all set." Her voice pulled Alistar back to the present.

"Thank you, lovey," Alistar said. "Say, I have heard some rumours of magnificent old paintings here. Have you see any?"

"All over the place. Look around."

Alistar grabbed his room key off the counter. "Thanks."

Beautifully varnished logs hugged together, making the hallway a sight to behold. The knots in the wood stood out like hazel eyes keeping watch. The auburn red carpet accented the walls nicely as Alistar walked toward his room. The lock clicked as Alistar unlocked the door. He was met with a fresh linen smell and pristine sheets pressed against the mattress. Decades of memories baked into the walls comforted Alistar and gave him a sense of peace that this would finally be where he could finish his composition.

The varnish glistened on his cello as he pulled it from its case. The voice of Mr. Portello, the man who'd nurtured Alistar's gift, echoed in his head. "Remember, boy, the painting holds the answers. The music is in the art. The music . . . is in the art." Alistar set his cello against its holder, standing proud just as Mr. Portello had.

Alistar unzipped the pocket of his suitcase and removed Mr. Portello's small black notebook. The ribbon marked a page in the middle of the book. The page was filled with hastily written notes.

Alistar flipped through the notebook until he came to a page with a crudely drawn picture in blue pen, mimicking a Picasso style scene of mountains, a lake, and the night sky. This was Mr. Potello's drawing of the painting, or at least what he could remember from the story he was told. Alistar ran his finger over the drawing, remembering the first time Mr. Portello told his story.

"Listen here, boy. This painting was done by one of the greatest artists to ever live, Savario. His work is transformational. You study his work and see the painting translate to music. He was one of our greatest allies as artists. He understood us. This painting has never been translated and you, my boy, are the one to translate it." Mr. Portello's voice was as clear in Alistar's head now as it was the first time he told the story.

Alistar grimaced as his abs tightened, signalling to him he had forgotten to eat during his whole day of travel. He remembered seeing signs for the dining hall when he was checking in. He grabbed his wallet, putting it into the pocket of his baggy balloon pants as he walked out the door.

It was quite a grand sight to enter into the lobby. Alistar found the dining room off the lobby. He stood at the 'Please Wait To Be Seated' sign, looking at the paintings along the wall.

"Hi," said a server who emerged from a door with a tray. "Feel free to take a table by the window."

"Awesome. I'm Alistar." He threw up a peace sign with

his fingers as he sat down at the table.

She reciprocated with a head nod and an awkward side smile. "Celina. What can I get you?"

"Can I help myself to the bagels in that display?"

"Absolutely. Go ahead."

A young woman in lodge uniform sat at a table against the wall. As Celina passed her, she said, "Grace, do you remember the other day you said you were missing the mop with the worn-in grip and black label on it?"

"Yeah! Did you see it?" Her friend gleamed in return.

"I did. It was in that storage closet by the service door. I moved the old painting so I could hang up my coat and there it was."

Alistar stopped chewing his bagel.

"That thing is always falling over and blocking something," Grace sighed. "I should have thought to check there."

"I don't know why they don't just toss it if they're not going to hang it on a wall." The girl leaned back in her chair, resting her hands down on her legs.

Alistar leaned forward, intrigued.

Grace took a sip of her coffee. "That thing has been haunting this place for years. My mom said Maxine always claimed it was cursed, but Duke can't throw it out because it was special to his grandmother, or something like that."

"I am sorry to interrupt. The name is Alistar," he said abruptly.

Both ladies turned to him. "You said earlier, yes."

"That painting has so much history with it. It can't be

thrown out. It's a masterpiece!" Alistar's inflection raised an octave.

Grace and Celina looked at him.

Grace shook her head. "You don't even know what painting we're talking about. How do you know it's valuable? There are hundreds of old paintings in this building." She waved a hand around the dining room, indicating the dozen paintings on the interior walls. "Artists used to come here all the time, and a lot of them paid for their stay with paintings because old Mrs. Laurel loved art and," she smirked, "as you can imagine, there are a *lot* of walls here."

Alistar leaned back into his chair, thinking.

Celina started back to the kitchen, but paused as she passed his table. "If you want to find your painting, talk to Daphne. I'll bet she'll know where you should look, and she'll probably sell it to you if you find it. Lord knows they need the money."

Alistar dropped his partially eaten bagel onto the plate, his stomach churning with the news, wishing cello paid better.

10.
At the Lodge

Maxine

Maxine tripped on the bottom step of the Lodge stairs and fell on top of her suitcase, cracking the hard shell. "Fuck." She picked herself up and muttered, "The gift that keeps on giving. This place is cursed." Her nostrils flared in disgust when she saw the broken plank that tripped her up. She took pictures from every angle, then half-stomped, half-limped into the lobby, empty of anyone—including an employee behind the desk.

The scent of polish and old wood jarred her back to those miserable days.

She hit the bell and waited. Nothing. She rang it again, then turned and leaned her back on the reception desk as she looked around. She checked the paintings, looking for the super ugly one she had cursed every time she walked by when she lived here.

There was a faded rectangle that showed what she suspected was its former location. She wondered if it had been moved for renovations or if someone had finally tossed it in the garbage, as she turned back to the desk and gave the bell another sharp smack.

There were lights on in the dining room, so she stepped and called out, "Hello, is anyone here?"

Her own voice echoed back. Her eyes fixated on the roped-off feature wall that housed the largest print of the dreaded house art, as she'd referred to it. It was gone too, or at least the frame was—or maybe it was turned into wallpaper or being decoupaged to the wall. But, it was the same damn hideous scene of the looming mountains and the treacherous lake, still annoying her decades after her escape from this misery. Now there was a portrait of a beaming young man and a cello beside it. How weird.

A young woman came down the stairs. Her wet hair indicated she was fresh from a shower. She moved behind the counter. "I'm so sorry. I hope you haven't been waiting long. What can I do for you?"

Maxine turned at the voice and their eyes connected, then froze in mutual astonishment.

"Daphne, what are you doing here?"

"More like, what are you doing here . . . Mom?"

Maxine took a deep breath and bit the inside of her cheek, nightmare scenarios of Daphne being ruined by the Lodge racing through her mind.

"Your grandfather is in hospital. He had a heart attack. I need to stay for a few days. What's your reason?"

"I've been helping Dad. He's been having a hard time— not that you would care."

"Daphne. That's not fair."

Daphne blinked. "He had a stroke, Mom. He's too young to have a stroke, isn't he?"

Maxine tilted her head and pondered what would be the best motherly gesture to comfort her daughter. She held her arms open. "Do you need a hug?"

Daphne came out from behind the counter. Maxine loosely wrapped her arms around her, uncertain of where to place her hands. She patted Daphne's back a few times then crumbled and held on tight. "It is so good to see you, my girl."

Daphne stiffened and pulled back. "Is Grandpa okay?'

"I'm not sure. He didn't wake up while I was there."

"Do you think I can go see him?"

"Please do. I'm sure he would like that. Could I register before you go?"

"Really?"

Maxine sighed. "Yes."

"Which room would you like? All three suites are free at the moment."

"I'll take the corner suite. Room 206 if you're offering. If it's still the same, it should have the biggest work area for me to spread out my files."

"Still can't leave work for a second, huh?" Daphne raised her eyebrows, then slid the key across the counter. "Excellent choice. Best views of the lake and garden. We can fill out the paperwork later."

Maxine hauled her suitcase to the elevator. She considered the odds of it working properly and how much of a risk getting inside would be. She would hate to be stranded in an elevator. The stairs are a sure thing even if it was a bitch to drag a suitcase up two rickety flights. But as it turned out, the elevator worked just fine.

She stepped into the familiar space, set her laptop bag

on the desk, and looked around. How many times had she made up this room? Hundreds, maybe a thousand times. Too many, at any rate.

Maxine walked out to the balcony, and looked out at the turquoise lake nestled in a forest of laurel trees and evergreens. The air was scented with resin. She had never understood Laurel Lake's appeal when she was growing up here, maybe because she saw it every day.

She'd been born with a desire to escape to the action and excitement of anywhere but here, a city girl, raised in the rural hamlet of Bored to Death. She joked about this in university. And then Duke, fourth year, worldly god of philosophical discussions held late into the night, had sucked her back here, right into his world.

She'd fallen hard. Hard enough to lose herself in his dreams, the fantasy world he created. He could talk a good talk. His ability to follow through on his grand schemes was not so great.

For maybe the first time in her life, Maxine did more than glance at the lake and surrounding scenery. She slowly and purposefully took it all in, inhaling the freshness of recently rained upon greenery, allowing the sun to warm her face. And, for the first time since the phone call, her heart stopped racing. The hammering in her chest lightened.

She stood, tears streaming down her cheeks, staring at the reflections of the trees on the glassy lake, and began to bargain with the universe to let her dad live a little longer with good health. *I will do anything, even If I have to live here at Laurel Lake. I'm not ready to say goodbye. If there is a god or angels or some energy healing miracle, please please help my dad.*

As she climbed into the bed, Maxine rolled her eyes at the print hanging above the headboard. It was the damned picture that had caused countless arguments with Duke and his fantasy world. Duke claimed it was a replica of a masterpiece created by Savario. She had asked Duke so many times, "Why would a famous artist come to this hellhole?"

As she drove back to the hospital, she wondered if there was still a print of it in every room. The tourists loved them and bought many posters back in her day. Occasionally, a lodge guest would steal one of the framed pictures. She would have gladly given them all away if Duke had let her.

- - - - -

Contrary to the nurse's prediction that morning, Maxine's father was not awake when she returned in the afternoon after a few hours of sleep.

"Is he going to be okay?" she asked the nurse who came in.

"We can't say for sure. It could go either way at this point. But the fact that he made it through the night is promising. Do you know if he has a power of attorney or a living will and where you could find them? They will be important as the family makes decisions regarding his care."

"He has both," Maxine nodded. She was thankful she'd made him take care of all that legal work no one ever wants to think about. "He was adamant about not wanting to be kept alive by artificial means."

"Can you bring those documents in, and do you have any other questions?"

"Not that I can think of. I'll get the documents this morning."

The nurse walked up to the bed and squeezed her dad's hand. "Good afternoon, Robert. Your daughter's here to see you." She turned to Maxine and smiled with compassion. "We're going to be here with him for about half an hour, if you want to grab a bite to eat or a coffee next door and perhaps pick up a book to pass the time?"

She understood the underlying message that her dad needed some privacy. "Thank you. I'll do that."

Maxine returned to the room with a box of files to work on, her dad's legal documents, a sickeningly sweet coffee, and enough snacks to feed both of them for a week. After a long day with no sign of consciousness from her dad, Maxine returned to Laurel Lodge for the evening.

11.
A clean slate

Grace Taylor

Grace Taylor closed the service door behind her and signed in on the housekeeping board. Every morning it hurt a bit to see her name on the board below her mom's. It had been months since Louise had been at work. Today there was a new name on the board: Christopher. Good. She could use some help.

Grace hung her backpack up, took off her coat, and tucked her car keys into an inside pocket in her pack. The ugly old painting stored on the floor of the closet tipped forward, and she pushed it back and wedged it in against a bucket.

Her car had started all right this morning, and the side mirror that had fallen off for the third time actually clicked back on the first try. That had to be a good omen for a better day.

Following the scent of coffee, she headed to the kitchen.

"Good morning, Chef. How are things?" Grace poured herself a cup of coffee as Chef plated eggs, bacon, and pancakes.

He grunted at her. "How do you think! The top oven isn't working again, there is still a leak in the fridge, and I'm almost out of milk."

"Oh, wow, that's a lot. Does Duke know?" She remembered too late Duke wasn't there. "I mean, did you tell Daphne?"

"Of course. 'We have to wait' she said. I've had it up to here." He waved his hands wildly around his head. "Broken equipment! Dying boss! If things don't change soon, I am leaving. Friends in Calgary are telling me about openings in restaurants. I've warned Daphne."

Grace backed out of the kitchen with her coffee. *Dying boss?* Yikes. Once Chef was in a mood, nothing was going to change it, and she wouldn't have her potentially good day spoiled by a grumpy grown toddler in a kitchen.

Looking over the list of occupied rooms, Grace thought about how busy the Lodge had been before the floods. Two years ago summer had brought with it rains, and the supposedly secure banks of the Laurel River had given way. The main floor had been the worst affected. It had filled with over a metre of water that had left mud and silt behind when it drained away.

The staff had all pitched in, of course, and for six months they were all positive the Lodge would recover.

Then the problems started to pile up, from cracked floor tiles to unsafe wiring. Staff members had left until only a few remained. Two were her mom and Leeroy.

Leeroy was older than her, but he had always been kind when she'd spent long hours at the Lodge while her mom worked. He could easily have ignored a lonely little girl. Instead, he called her Gracie, showed her how things like doorknobs worked, and let her follow him around when he was doing easy tasks. It had been comforting to find Leeroy was still at the Lodge when she returned to take over her mother's job.

Grace had been living in Calgary, attending college, when Louise Taylor collapsed one morning at work, leading to months of medical tests. Multiple Sclerosis was the diagnosis. They had hoped Louise would go into remission and she would recover, but she hadn't yet. Now she was in a wheelchair most of the time, and doctors said they needed to prepare for the worst.

Since her dad's death when she was ten, it had been just her and her mom. Louise had worked hard to give Grace as many opportunities as possible. Grace adored her mother and they had become best friends, as well as mother and daughter. After the initial shock of the diagnosis, Grace decided she needed to be at home to care for her mom and left the big city and her dreams behind.

Living in Laurel Lake hadn't been what she had planned for her life, but she would look for the positives in her new life, like the pleasure of spending more time with her mom,

"Grace, mia bella!"

Grace looked up to see the Italian waitress coming toward her.

"Thank goodness you are here. I couldn't listen to that bear in the kitchen anymore!"

Grace hugged Celina as she bounced into the back office.

"Remember what the blue fish said, 'Just keep swimming'!"

Celina snickered. Grace had needed a friend when she started working at the Lodge. She and Celina had both found themselves somewhere they hadn't planned to be and had become close friends, discovering a shared love of Keanu Reeves and a hatred of mosquitos.

"Did you get your paper done, Grace? I was worried you would be up all night."

"I did, and I even got to bed by one!"

The assignment had been a midterm paper for a bookkeeping class, a subject Grace liked. The challenge was completing all her classwork, caring for her mom, and working full-time at the Lodge. With only a year left to complete, she was determined to get her degree in accounting, continuing her studies remotely. That was the easy bit, she knew. Once she graduated, she needed a job that would pay well enough to support both her and her mother while allowing her to stay at Laurel Lake. Ah well, she thought, I'll cross that bridge when I get to it.

Grace reached into her jeans pocket for a hair tie and pulled her light brown hair into a ponytail. "I saw a new name on the board. Who's Christopher?"

Celina rolled her eyes. "Just a kid. He's still in high school, so he can only work weekends. He thinks he's going to be a great writer. When he was doing kitchen orientation he was writing in a notebook like some kind of spy."

Grace laughed, "Don't spies just memorize everything so there's no evidence?"

Celina shrugged, turning to see if anyone was standing at the 'Please Wait To Be Seated' sign.

Grace took a deep breath. "Okay, my break is finished. No more excuses: it's linen time!"

"That means I have to clear the dining room. Unless you want dirty plates?"

Celina winked as Grace headed out of the door.

In a guest room, shaking out a clean flat sheet, Grace breathed in the fresh linen scent. It was one of her favourite smells, connected as it was to memories of her mom and the laughing camaraderie of her efficient housekeeping teams through Grace's childhood. She chuckled, thinking that it wasn't quite as fun when the housekeeping team was just one person.

She quickly and efficiently made the bed up before cleaning the ensuite bathroom, One of the features she loved about the Lodge was the clawfoot tubs in each bathroom. They were beautiful and added charm and class to each suite at a time when so many modern hotels were scrapping baths in favour of showers. The character of the Lodge was special, and if it could be restored to its former glory until it brimmed with guests again, it would benefit the whole town.

Expanding the housekeeping team to two would be a start. She looked forward to training Christopher. She hoped he'd be a good worker.

Later in the day, Grace was in the lobby polishing the frame of a large landscape painting when there was a loud bang followed by raised voices coming from the kitchen.

There was a crash and the reverberating smash of a slammed door.

Grace dropped her polishing rag on a table and rushed through the kitchen door, entering just behind Celina.

Daphne was standing surrounded by broken crockery, with her hands over her eyes. She was swaying and making alarming wimpering noises.

"Daphne! What happened? Are you okay?"

Daphne looked up, her face pale, her eyes bleak. "We just lost our chef! I don't know what to do. This is not going to work. Nothing I can do is making a difference, and even when something does seem to go well, you can guarantee that it will be followed by another disaster."

"Oh dear," said Grace. "Let me make you some tea. My mother swears it solves all problems."

Daphne smiled shakily. "She does, doesn't she? She made me a lot of tea when I was a teenager."

Celina said, "I will make it. You both sit." She swept them out into the dining room and disappeared back into the kitchen.

Daphne stared blankly at the old landscape paintings around the room. They came in so many different sizes. So many different treatments of trees, mountains, Laurel Lake, and the Lodge itself.

Grace watched the kitchen door until Celina returned with three little steel teapots and three teacups and saucers on a tray, with three packets of shortbread from the restaurant supplier.

"Here," said Grace, pushing the sugar bowl toward Daphne. "When you've had a shock, a strong sugary tea is best."

Daphne obediently spooned sugar into her mug.

As Daphne sipped her tea, Grace whispered to Celina, "I don't suppose you can cook?" Someone had to make the meals while Daphne looked for a new chef.

Celina swallowed. "Not really. How about you?"

Grace shook her head, wondering if maybe her mom could come in for a while. Though her MS made it difficult to do the physically demanding tasks required by housekeeping, perhaps with a stool to lean on she could cook for a couple of hours? The Lodge wasn't very busy these days. It might work. She could ask.

Daphne sighed and set down her mug. "Thank you. Tea and a break were just what I needed. I hadn't realized things had gotten so bad. It's obvious that Dad has been missing things for months. I don't know if bills have been paid because the office is a mess, and invoices and receipts are scattered all over his desk. I can't find any bank statements." She sniffed and wiped at her eye. 'The only thing I am sure of is that he never did any online banking because 'computers are the devil's creation!'"

Grace couldn't cook, but she could help with this problem. "I've just finished my courses on bookkeeping. Would you like me to take a look and see what I can do to organize things?" Grace asked.

Daphne stared at her. "Could you really? Do you have the time?"

Grace didn't really. Not with her course, but it was almost done and this would be career experience she could put on a resumé. It was an investment for her future. She nodded. "I can do it if I stay longer for a few afternoons, or I could come in the evening for a few hours."

Daphne took a deep breath. "Yes, please, Grace. We'll get Christopher to cover housekeeping when you're bookkeeping. That would be an enormous help. I need to find Dad's legal documents like his medical directive, so I can take care of things. Can you keep an eye out for them?"

Grace nodded. "We'll get through this, Daphne, don't worry."

12.
I have to what?

Celina Cavallero

Nineteen-year-old Celina Cavallero collapsed onto a blue faded couch and closed her dark, tired eyes. She set her phone for a twenty-minute break—her first in nearly five hours serving tables at the Laurel Lake Lodge Restaurant. Daphne and Leeroy had moved this couch to the back service hall to make room for floor repairs in the lobby and it was an ideal place to hide. Sliding over an enormous old painting to hide her from anyone not looking too closely, Celina pushed her dark hair out of her eyes and stretched out her short frame.

When Celina had arrived at the Lodge from Turin, ready to start her grand year of adventure working and travelling in Canada, she'd been shocked to find her new place of employment was an isolated, nearly deserted lodge with burst pipes and an unreliable heating system.

Now that Chef had quit, it was up to Celina to fill breakfast orders while Leeroy did the serving, looking awkward and miserable out of his overalls.

Having never cooked much at home, Celina found every order to be an inscrutable puzzle—only with more accidents and embarrassment. *When is bacon cooked through? Which tools are heat resistant and which ones fill your sauté pans with strands of melted plastic? How do you flip a pancake, and do they always stay raw on the inside just out of spite?*

By mid-morning, Daphne came into the kitchen to ask why they had "run out" of fried eggs and were only serving scrambled. Celina had not managed to plate a single fried egg without breaking the yolk.

"I don't know how to cook!" Celina sniffled. "I'm doing my best!"

Daphne wrapped her arms around her. "I'm so sorry, Celina. I know you are. Let's take hot meals off the menu for now. Can you handle baking muffins and scones, perhaps? Maybe making some sandwiches?"

Celina nodded.

"I appreciate this more than I can say. I've got an ad in the Calgary Herald and at the unemployment office, but there haven't been any applicants yet. Thank you for helping us get through this!"

- - - - -

The next morning, a soft alarm buzzed on Celina's phone, and she reluctantly got up. Every bone in her short frame provided an opinion about moving. Who knew that a kitchen job would be such a workout?

As Celina approached the back stairs of the Lodge, she saw Daphne talking to Leeroy.

Daphne stood with one hand on her hip and the other massaging her temple. With his shoulders hunched and hands in his pockets, Leeroy looked as though he wanted to be any place but here.

Drawing closer but still out of sight, Celina heard

Daphne ask, " . . . and what about the burst pipes?"

"What about them?"

"That isn't something we can handle ourselves."

Leeroy muttered, "Well, maybe if I just patched . . ."

Daphne interrupted with a sigh so deep that it appeared to also release the last vestiges of her self-restraint. "No, Leeroy. No more patching." Her voice dropped lower. "We need to hire some outside help, and I think I found just the crew."

Leeroy inhaled sharply. "Outside help? You don't have the money!"

"Let me worry about that. Using professionals tends to save money in the long run."

Leeroy's jaw clenched. "I see how it is."

"I'm not firing you," Daphne said. "I ran into Jared Nelson the other day."

"Jared Nelson?" Leeroy's eyes widened. "Mr. Laurel would never . . ."

"Well, Mr. Laurel doesn't know everything, and he isn't making those decisions right now," Daphne snapped back.

Leeroy's eyes narrowed with disdain. "Well, Mr. Laurel knows something about loyalty."

"If you say so," Daphne replied as she walked away.

13.
Underbaked

Leo

Although he had been at the Laurel Lake Lodge for several days, his view had been strictly what he could see out the window or the landscape painting on the wall above the bed.

His exploration of the Lodge consisted only of running to and from the vending machine in pyjamas twice a day. When his stomach growled that particular morning he realized with an involuntary gag that he could not bear to eat another bag of vending machine chips.

Leo changed into khaki pants and a button-down shirt, and meandered down the hallway, slightly embarrassed when he took a wrong turn and nearly bumped into a member of the housekeeping staff.

Leo stood in the empty dining room beside the 'Please Wait To Be Seated' sign for an age before a server pushed open the kitchen door, carrying a tray loaded down with baked goods.

"Oh!" she said in a lovely accent. "I am sorry. I did not see you there. Please sit where you like. Can I bring you coffee?"

"Yes. Is there a dinner special?"

She smiled somewhat wearily. "No, I'm sorry. Our chef recently quit. We can only offer muffins and scones at the moment. The apple scone is particularly tasty. I can warm one up for you."

"That sounds good. Is there a place in town where I can find some protein later?" He tried to not to look like he was complaining.

"There's a burger place by the highway and a pub called The Roadkill Café. Be warned, It gets rowdy there by about eight."

"All right. I'll think about that later. Warm scone for now." He studied the room while he waited. A dozen tables for four. Half a dozen for two. Sixty seats. If it was full, that was a busy dining room for a single chef, but with a sous-chef it'd be just right. It was a beautiful setting with the lake and mountain views out the windows. A good chef could make this a destination dining location for the region. It didn't sound like there was any competition around.

When the server set down the huge scone with tiny ramekins of butter and jam on the side, he leaned over it to inhale the heavenly scents of cinnamon, cloves, and apples. "This looks wonderful. Thank you."

"Can I get you anything else?"

He pondered asking for a job application, but that meant facing life without Ana and being responsible to all these people. He'd inevitably let them all down. "No," he said. "Nothing." As she turned away he studied the scone, which looked suspiciously underbaked.

14.
Drive safely

Grace

Two days later, a storm had blown in, and Grace had had one of the worst days at work she could remember. Her car did not want to start, so she was late. Although they now had a new chef, the problems with appliances hadn't been solved, so there was no coffee waiting, as the coffee maker had decided to die.

Even Celina was not her chirpy self, having had to walk through the wind and snow to get to the Lodge that morning.

They found a kettle in a cupboard and made some instant coffee Celina considered to be a crime against real coffee. The heating in the Lodge was doing its best but the guest rooms were chilly, so Grace had dug out extra blankets to put in each room. By the end of the day, she was cold and tired and not looking forward to the drive home. She hoped her car, parked out of the wind, would start.

Ten minutes after going out to turn it on and get it warmed up, Grace gave in and cried. It was dead to the world; she couldn't afford to get it fixed this month, and the cost of a cab would eat into her weekly grocery budget.

Returning to the back hallway, she sat on the bench and blew her nose.

Leeroy pushed through the door to the kitchen. He sat

beside her. His voice was soft when he finally said, "Hey, Gracie."

"Hey," she replied with a sniffle.

"What's got you so upset?"

Grace stared into her lap. "My car won't start. I can't afford to get it fixed or even towed to the garage. I don't know what to do. I can usually find a way to deal with a problem, but this time I have no idea."

Leeroy rubbed his chin. "I'm not a mechanic, but I could take a look at your car if you like?"

"Yes, please, Leeroy, that would be awesome!"

Grace gave him a watery smile. "I'll just go check the linen closet."

Grace stood in the linen closet, staring at the perfectly aligned stacks of sheets, thankful for privacy. She didn't hold out much hope that Leeroy would be able to get the car started, but it meant a great deal to her that he had offered to help. She had friends, but there were times she felt very alone. Sometimes working at the Lodge reminded her of being a little girl, having to go to work with her mother, wishing there were other kids to play with.

Leeroy had always been there, she realized. She had loved watching him mend broken things around the Lodge. He had been kind and patient, willing to answer her many questions and happy to let her follow him around. Now, Leeroy was taking care of her once again.

Grace heard the service door open and close. Leeroy stood at the entrance to the linen closet, brushing snow off his sleeves.

"Did you have any luck?"

He grinned at her.

"Gracie, someone or something is looking out for us, because I got that car going."

Grace squealed and lunged into his arms "Thank you," she said, squeezing him tightly, "Thank you so much. You are a genius!"

Leeroy laughed. "I left it running, so go on and head home. Call me if you get stuck. I'll come and get you in the truck. And text me when you get home, okay? If it doesn't start tomorrow, I can come and pick you up. It'll be okay."

She stood on tiptoe to kiss his cheek.

"Thanks for always being here."

Leeroy blushed scarlet and waved at the door. "Go on with you. Drive safely."

15.
Not Okay

Leo

The next day, Leo walked down a trail on the Lodge grounds. The sun reflected brilliantly off the snow, and he rubbed at his eyes, annoyed at himself for not packing sunglasses to protect from glare.

He kept hearing Ana's voice, replaying her departure, hearing the door shutting behind her.

His sleeping patterns had altered drastically lately. Now he slept less rather than more. That meant he had more time to consider all his mistakes and the futility of having any dreams when dreams could not come true.

Overwhelmed with weariness, he took refuge on a small bench along the trail and slumped over, resting both elbows on his thighs. Leo could not recall the last time he cried in his numb passage through the days, and was surprised when he saw tears drop onto his khaki trousers.

His body felt too heavy. Keeping himself upright felt a nearly impossible task. He dropped onto his knees. The anguish he had been trying desperately to keep locked inside came out in raspy breaths. Painful sobs gurgled and screeched from his throat. Exhausted, Leo fell forward, watching his hands sink roughly into the snow. Poised on all fours like a beast, he let his head hang between his broad shoulders as the cold bit knees and hands and wet eyes. He relished the pain.

In intervals, Leo's breath slowed, but then another wave of pain assaulted him and fresh tears fell.

He didn't know how long he'd been like that when crunching snow behind him paused. He remained perfectly still. He felt a sharp sting as he bit his lip to try and control himself as he prayed whoever was there would keep going.

There was a rustle of clothing and the bench creaked.

Fighting embarrassment, Leo hoisted himself back onto the bench. "Excuse me," he murmured. He kept his eyes on the pattern he'd made in the snow. In his peripheral vision, he could see that it was a man beside him. He was small in stature, but Leo thought they were probably the same age.

He said nothing. He just sat beside Leo on the bench.

Leo held his breath and tried to keep his shoulders from shaking. He ignored the searing burn in his chest.

As they sat, he realized just the silent companionship was helping. He began to hear the world around him: rustles from the trees, creaks from the ice, and distant voices from the Lodge.

"It is okay not to be okay," the man finally said in a gentle voice, free from pity. He simply stated it as a fact.

Leo lifted his head to look at the man, who met Leo's eyes solemnly.

"How can I help?"

Leo's face crumpled. "I could really use a hug," he said, knowing it was an absurd request of a stranger.

The man didn't respond immediately, but when he

turned his body and held out his arms, Leo wrapped himself around him.

The stark contrast in their sizes and the strangeness of the situation was awkward at first. The stranger was warm and wiry, despite his size. Leo buried his face into the man's shoulder while the stranger patted him between the shoulder blades, soothing his shaking body as he wept again. If the stranger felt discomfort, he did not show it, and the steady repetition of his voice repeating, "You'll be okay," were like a balm.

Gradually Leo pulled away and faced forward, looking to the lake. His eyes traced the outline of the mountain behind it and inhaled the scent of the pine trees.

They sat in comfortable silence, until at least Leo cleared his throat.

"Thank you," he said, trying to ward off the embarrassment that was creeping in. "I'm Leo."

"I'm Yize," the man said. "It was brave of you to face your pain."

"Brave?" Leo gave a rasping chuckle.

The man stared ahead. "Our world tells men that they shouldn't feel their emotions, and if they do, they should do so in silence." He shifted his body before adding, "But I don't think anybody should be alone when they're in pain. I am sorry if I intruded."

"No, thank you. I'm glad you did."

When the man turned to face him, Leo realized that Yize's eyes were wet. "After I experienced a great loss, I realized that while you feel less vulnerable hiding your feelings," he said with a wobbly smile, "nobody can help you if they don't know you need help. It was kind people who helped me with my grief. I am just passing it along."

Leo considered his words a while before he leaned back with a sigh. "I'm so glad you found me."

They sat for a while, alternating between Leo telling him the bare bones of his story and just sitting in comfortable silence, until the snow began to fall softly again.

"I should go back to the Lodge," Leo said. "I'm sorry for taking up so much of your time."

"It's not a problem. Look, I think you could really benefit from a professional. Promise me you'll find a local therapist so you can work through your grief with support?"

Leo nodded.

At the parking lot, Leo thanked Yize and went up to his room. A phone notification beeped and he pulled his phone from his pocket. The background photo was Anastasia and him smiling at each other on a weekend trip two summers ago.

It was time to accept that Ana was never coming back. Leo wished her a silent goodbye as he deleted the photo from his wallpaper and reset it with a picture of Laurel Lake.

He wanted to complete his walk, but he should get some dry clothes on so he didn't get hypothermia. If he was going to live, he needed to look after himself.

16.
Scouting

Yize Peng

Yize Peng had no particular place to be tonight and he was dressed for the weather, so he was content to make another circuit of Laurel Lake to ponder the beauty of the place and the opportunities it might have, despite the falling snow.

He'd been driving down the highway after a trip to check out potential locations to bring tour groups, when he'd seen a sign for Laurel Lake Lodge. While the sign had been a bit dilapidated, the area had the type of jaw-dropping scenery that tourists to Canada loved, so he figured he'd check it out. He hadn't planned to check in, but after spending a couple of hours supporting that young man through his crisis, he thought he should probably spend the night rather than driving through a snowy night.

He was comfortable in his winter gear, and the trail around the lake was well-beaten, despite the snow. It was obviously popular. The air was invigorating, scented with evergreens. If only he could bottle the feeling of breathing in that scent, he'd make a fortune.

Yize strode along the trail in the waning light, thinking it was a much nicer experience than yesterday, when he had unlocked the door to the office of Canada Far & Wide, and stepped into the silence of early morning.

A familiar sight had welcomed him inside, walls covered in posters of white sandy beaches, sunsets over cityscapes, cruise liners atop glassy blue oceans, and plush pillows on king sized beds overlooking a variety of vistas. The five desks all faced the large windowed frontage, so he and his work colleagues met clients with forward-facing smiles. A glass partition separated Mr. Hodgkins' manager's office from everyone else.

Yize had let his imagination glimpse himself sitting in that office behind the impressive desk, organizing his staff and plucking the more select venues for himself. With a new successful venue to his name, he would achieve his dream of promotion and take that very desk as his own. He was so close to it now, he sometimes found it difficult to sleep, hence his early morning arrival at the office.

Since it was hours before opening, he turned to lock the door behind him and then sat at the nearest desk to the front door. The sun wasn't up yet, but that was fine.

This was his domain, fastidiously organized and clean, every pen lined up and brochures categorized by area. He knew at a glance when someone walked through the door what vacation experience they were looking for. This gave him an advantage over his colleagues as he would smile and say, "It's the beach or the city escape or the hiking tour you are interested in, is it?" It was rare that he was incorrect. The clients would come sit on the other side of his desk, exclaiming, "Yes! How did you know?"

Of course, this skill meant he was increasingly unpopular with his office counterparts James, Sandi, and

Celia, but not with Mr. Hodgkins, who praised his skill when he patted Yize's back and told his other staff to take note. "Take a leaf out of Yize's book and learn to identify your clients. It is the path to success in this industry."

Yize ignored their jealousy and focused on his goal: branch manager. Mr. Hodgkins' early retirement was a gift and Yize was determined to take advantage. He hoped achieving such a position might ease his family's constant pressure to have a worthy profession. Of course, his parents and grandmother were of the view that only 'real' professions like medicine, engineering, or law were worth any time and effort.

Yize obligingly met their expectations throughout high school with straight A's and marks of excellence, but upon graduation he admitted he was pursuing another path. Not unexpectedly, his preferred choice of profession met with forceful opposition, especially from his paternal grandmother.

Nai Nai lived with him and his parents and was a force to be reckoned with, ruling the household from the first day she stepped through the front door. She instructed his mother on the correct way to prepare and cook traditional meals; they never ate Western food within the home. His father deferred to his mother in all things, which frustrated Yize, but he had never voiced those frustrations until the fateful day when his university acceptance letter arrived.

The envelope lay open on the supper table when he walked in the door.

"This is my mail. Who opened it?"

Nai Nai glared at him and smacked her hand on the

offending letter.

"You bring shame to the family, Yize. This is not a profession. You will change your course and follow in your father's footsteps as a lawyer."

Yize tried to explain his passion for travel, exploring the world, but he was met with disdain. For months he was met with silence and scorn. The family ate in the dining room, but he had to eat in the kitchen.

He tried explaining to his parents there was more choice in Canada and that success was achievable in many professions. But Nai Nai held a rigid power over them both. She scolded Yize every chance she got and pushed his father forward, telling him to make his son to put the family first, so he did not bring shame on them all.

The two months prior to entering university were distressing to everyone in the household. His mother lost weight. His father worked later and later into the evenings.

Yize retreated into himself. He made excuses to miss supper at home. His favourite escape was the main library, where he found books on tourism and studied them, making copious notes.

Yize was relieved when he could finally leave for university and escape the constant badgering. He viewed the ends of semesters with dread and delayed returning home whenever he could.

Even when he achieved a distinction in his Bachelor of Hospitality Management, their congratulations were muted at best. He hoped this promotion would sway his family's opinion.

He had taken the coffee pot and filled it up in the small kitchenette beside the manager's office and scooped coffee into the percolator. Returning to his desk, he opened a top desk drawer and took out his ledger-type notebook and opened it up, the two large pages spread before him. He scanned entries for the month, checking appointments, to do tasks, and follow up dates.

Having each task highlighted in a different colour ensured he never missed anything: green for follow up, pink for appointments, and blue for that day's calls. Today there was an extra colour—yellow—and excitement rose in his chest. Yellow signified a new venture, an opportunity to add to his already successful portfolio of niche hotels.

He used his days off to explore and hike, either with several of his university friends or alone. When he came across a new hotel or campsite he would chat with the owners, their staff, and the visitors to get a sense of the place. That led him to be driving down the highway when he'd seen the sign for Laurel Lake Lodge.

He'd completed the circuit of the lake as the snow had gotten thicker and the wind had started blowing. He stood in the parking lot, examining the lodge building through the blowing snow.

It was the type of rustic place that appealed to specific people searching for the experience of an older Canada. That type yearned to escape the urban crush, and were in love with the idea of the great Canadian wilderness, though they lack any ability to cope with the real thing. He could think of a few tour companies that would love to bring groups for the photo opportunities in the woods and around the lake. The mountains looming above the lake had been awe-inspiring, before the snow heavy clouds had obscured them.

Yes. Laurel Lake Lodge would be a perfect overnight space if they had nice rooms and a good dining room. He'd stay overnight and decide.

17.
Ensconced

Leo

An hour after Leo had left Yize Peng, he was back on another trail, thinking about walking into town to find the Roadkill Café.

Before long, the blustering wind was blowing the snow around and it clouded Leo's view of the world around him. The map had indicated it should take about twenty minutes to walk into town by this trail. It seemed like he'd been walking a lot longer than that. He checked his phone, and sure enough, forty-five minutes had passed since he'd left his room. This couldn't be the correct trail. He might be lost forever. He could freeze to death and not be found until spring. He didn't want to die. The irony made him laugh despite his fear. He couldn't think of anything to do but continue walking. A trail had to lead somewhere.

Leo almost let out a cry of relief upon seeing a little house up ahead. Pain shot through his nearly frozen hand as he rapped on the door. The door opened slowly, to reveal an elderly woman, roughly seventy or eighty, Leo guessed. She knit her eyebrows slightly upon seeing him, but, after quickly glancing behind him at the storm ravaging outside, she motioned him in.

He had only begun apologizing when the woman started

shushing him with a chuckle.

"Dear, don't you apologize. It's a right nightmare out there, and you'd have caught your death if you hadn't had the good sense to knock on my door."

Leo smiled with equal parts appreciation and sheepishness. He stood with his shoulders hunched, painfully aware his boots and jacket would soon form puddles on the floor beneath him.

"Take off those wet things and come on in. Put your boots in the tray. There are slippers in the basket."

He hung his coat on a hook and found a pair of crocheted slippers large enough to fit him.

"There now," she said as she coughed into her sleeve. "Let's get you something warm to drink. I'm Molly. Molly O'Shea."

"Leo Bouchard. I'm a guest up at Laurel Lake Lodge."

"Of course, you are." She smiled, relaxed and confident. Leo envied that.

Leo shuffled into the kitchen after Molly. A pile of cough lozenge wrappers were scattered on the counters and around her garbage can.

"Have a seat."

Molly started the gas stove and motioned for Leo to join her as they waited for the water to boil in a small blue kettle.

She cleared her throat, and a noise rattled in her chest as she began to make conversation.

"Are you all right?"

"Oh, I'm fine. Don't you worry. I'm not contagious."

She had just sat opposite him when the kettle whistled.

She gave a weary sigh, but before she could stand, Leo quickly jumped up. "I'll get that. You just sit. I don't want to be a bother." The Brown Betty teapot was on the counter and mugs were hanging on a mug tree behind it.

"Do you need milk?" she asked, with a wave at the fridge. "Just help yourself."

He expected to have to search for the milk in the fridge, but a nearly empty carton of milk was the only thing on the shelves. He gave it a surreptitious glance to confirm it was within date and brought it to the table. The sugar bowl and a spoon were already there.

They sat together drinking their tea, but Molly continued to cough into her handkerchief. "I'd offer you something to eat, but I don't cook so much any more. I've been going up to the Lodge, but their last chef departed in a blaze of self-absorption and I haven't stocked any groceries yet."

"Ah," said Leo. "Yes, I've been surviving on rocks masquerading as scones."

"Celina is a sweet girl, but she is definitely not a baker," she chuckled and then broke off with another cough.

Leo glanced at the weather app on his phone, and his eyes flicked to the window where the snow continued to fall heavily.

"Stay as long as you like, dear," Molly told him after interpreting his glance out the window. "I've got a guest room if you can't get back."

"Thank you," he replied. How kind people were in Laurel Lake. First Yize Peng and now Molly O'Shea.

He found himself ensconced in a lovely room, buried

beneath two quilts and three afghans. The little room even had a tiny ensuite. He slept better than he had in months.

The next morning, the snow had stopped. They shared another cup of tea. Then Leo trudged back to the Lodge with Molly's good wishes.

Once there, he retrieved his car keys and wallet, then headed to the grocery store in his rented car. The roads had been ploughed and he had no trouble on the drive.

It was nearly dark by the time he pulled into Molly's driveway, which had thick snow that hadn't yet been cleared. He made a mental note to return early the next morning and shovel it for her—with that cough and at her age, she definitely shouldn't be outside in this cold weather.

In the meantime, he shoveled the path to the door. When he was done, he knocked, listening for Molly's shuffling footsteps from inside. When the door opened, her face lit up in welcome surprise. "Leo!" she exclaimed. "What are you doing back here so soon?" She peered past him at his car. "You didn't get lost again, did you?"

He chuckled. It might have been the first time he'd laughed in a while, and the sound felt rusty, even to his own ears. "No, I didn't, ma'am," he replied. "But I came back with a few things. Do you mind if I return your kindness?"

"Whatever do you mean?" she asked. But then she pushed wide her door and gestured. "Come in, come in! Don't stand out there in the cold."

He grabbed the two grocery bags he'd set down on her porch and carried them inside. She noticed and asked curiously, "What's all that?"

"My surprise," he told her, smiling. "Would it be okay if I use your kitchen? I'd like to cook you a meal."

Molly shook her head, obviously bemused. "Of course. Help yourself."

She sat at the kitchen table as he unloaded the bags. He made himself at home in her kitchen and began chopping onions and getting out the various pots and pans he needed.

After watching him for a minute, Molly made as if to rise to her feet. "I shouldn't just be sitting here," she said, but he tutted at her.

"You just rest," he told her. "You've been kind enough. Now it's my turn to return the favour."

His obvious expertise as he threw pinches of herbs into a pot with the vegetables and sautéed chicken didn't stop Molly from inserting a few comments here and there. "Rinse the chicken in the sink," she told him.

He shook his head. "Definitely not. That's a good way to spread salmonella," he told her. "You should never rinse chicken. It should go from the package straight into the pan."

They argued a bit good-naturedly about cooking techniques, and Leo could see Molly was as stubborn as Anastacia had been. And, for once the thought of Ana didn't overwhelm him with grief. It was as if he'd used up his quota of sadness after crying at the lake.

When they sat down to eat, Molly took a deep breath of the steaming plate of food and her smile was huge. "This smells delicious," she told him. "Why, you should be a professional cook."

He didn't tell her that he had been. He simply grinned at her and said, "Bon appétit.

18.
This totally stinks

Celina

Ever since she'd overheard Daphne and Leeroy talking, Celina had been worrying. At first it was just a niggling concern, but every day she had more questions. Like, who was Jared Nelson? It seemed like Leeroy did not seem to like him at all. Leeroy seemed to like everyone. What was wrong with this Jared? The questions had grown into fears, like what was that about there not being enough money?

When she'd started working here, Celina had been grateful that the Lodge was slow and quiet. But what if the Lodge didn't have enough customers to stay open? What if they couldn't pay her wages? Would she have to end her trip early and return home?

Celina's face burned at the thought of the humiliation.

She just imagined what everyone would say:

Oh, our little Celina could not survive big, scary Canada with all the bears.

Oh, our little Celina does not know how to make any money.

Oh, our little Celina. How pathetic.

Celina had fantasized about Canada since reading *Anne of Green Gables* in English class. She had imagined visiting Canada—walking across red sandy beaches in a puffed-sleeved dress and picnicking with raspberry cordial. Canada had always been an imaginary vacation she could take any time they wanted.

When she'd learned that Italy had an international work exchange program for eighteen to thirty-year-olds she was overjoyed. She could have chosen New Zealand, the UK, or many other countries, but Celina was determined to go to Canada. She planned to leave right after graduation and spend a year working, travelling, and having adventures in the place where Anne Shirley and Diana Barry had been epic best friends.

She accepted a job at the romantic sounding Laurel Lake Lodge in Alberta's Kananaskis country.

Celina had not realized how far Laurel Lake was from Prince Edward Island.

"Oh, yes, Europeans often underestimate how big Canada is and how much more effort and money it takes to travel," the program coordinator laughingly explained, most unhelpfully, after Celina had arrived. "No, we don't have as many budget airlines or high-speed trains as they have in Europe."

Celina groaned, remembering the conversation.

And now, here she was, in a hotel that might close, failing at . . . Oh, the muffins!

Celina lurched toward the oven door, pulled it open, and then fell back to avoid the roaring miasma of smoke and heat.

"What's going on? Oh! Celina, are you all right?" Daphne helped Celina back on her feet.

"I'm sorry. I ruined the muffins."

Daphne sighed, "That's all right. Apparently, I'm ruining things, too. Just open a window, and then bring table six an order of Irish breakfast and some scones."

Celina glanced at the scones dubiously, "Irish breakfast?"

"It's a tea." Daphne pointed at the tin on the back counter. "Not many people order it, but Dad always has some on hand for Molly O'Shea."

Bringing out the order, Celina saw Daphne seated across from an elderly woman with soft white hair who wore a crocheted hat with flowers and a matching cardigan. Where had she seen that hat before?

"Celina, have you met Molly? Come over and introduce yourself."

"Hello, Molly. I'm your server today. Welcome to the Laurel Lake Lodge Restaurant."

"Laurel Lake Lodge Restaurant? Daphne, I like the sound of that. Maybe you're doing better than you think. Nice to meet you, Celina. Maybe I should welcome you, since I've been coming to the Lodge for years and you're quite new."

Molly smiled warmly, perfectly at ease with herself and without one bit of the stress and tension the Lodge folks had showing on her lined face.

Suddenly more relaxed herself, Celina laughed, "Well, I hope I won't have to compete with you for my job, then."

Molly and Daphne joined with chuckles.

"I hear you've come to us all the way from Italy. How are you finding the Canadian winter?" Molly asked.

"In my city, Turin, it rarely snows, even though we are close to the Alps. We just have a lot of rain and maybe, at the coldest, it is negative three degrees Celsius." She glanced out the window and gave an involuntary shiver.

"Well, this is different then. I hope you have the right kind of coat and hat, dear."

"I think my coat and hat are all right, but I did find it very slippery on the road." Celina realized where she'd seen Molly's crocheted hat. "Oh, you must live in that cute cottage on Laurel Lake Road! I saw your hat in the window on my way to work this morning."

"I do! My, what sharp eyes you must have. We likely walked that same path today," Molly affirmed.

"But didn't you find it slippery on the way here?" Celina asked, mystified that a woman her grandmother's age could manage so well on the icy roads and walkways.

Molly smiled, "I'm fine, dear. I've walked that way my whole life. At this time of year, all you need are some ice cleats." Molly reached into her pockets and pulled out a handful of black rubber with metal spikes. "You see? You put them onto your winter boots." She mimed the action. "Of course, you have to take them off when you come inside, but outside, these will bite into ice and keep you from sliding on the trails."

Celina looked at the little rounded tips doubtfully.

"You'll find them at that store that Felix's son runs. What do they call the place now, Daphne?"

"Outdoor Recreation Centre," Daphne responded with a smile.

"That's right. Ask for Felix. He'll help you."

- - - - -

Celina carefully eased the rubber frame of the ice cleats over her boots. The following morning, since she didn't start until eleven, she'd headed off in her quest for ice cleats. Finding the store using Molly's directions had proven to be its own challenge, since 'Just across from the big spruce with the blue bird house, down the road from the gas station' wasn't something she could look up on her phone. Still, once Celina was there, the salesperson, who turned out to be Felix's granddaughter, had helped her find a pair quickly. Success!

Walking down the wooded path around the lake, Celina found that she was secure on the trail where previously she had been skidding. Steadier on her feet, Celina began to admire the morning sun filtering through the trees. The area around the lake was, in fact, beautiful—not as amazing as Avonlea, Celina believed with conviction—but full of soft pockets of rosy morning light.

As she approached the Lodge, Celina felt increasingly confident. She spotted a low-lying branch covered in snow and decided to pull it back. Before, she would have simply walked around it, but today, why not? With unthinking ease, Celina released the branch. A great clump of snow sprayed forward. Celina laughed with satisfaction as the clumps of snow hurdled forward, until she noticed that one rather large clump was sailing toward a small crowd of furry creatures—some black and some white.

As the snow landed among them and they scurried away from it, Celina quickly realized that they were not a group of animals with black or white fur. Rather, each creature had both black and white fur. How cute they were with their black bodies with broad white stripes outlining their backs, big fluffy tails, and waddling gaits!

"Hello, you adorable animals!" she laughed, stepping forward, and reaching into her pocket for her phone. This would be something to impress Giulia. Their hair was even more impressive than Paulo's!

The largest of the animals made a funny hissing noise and stamped its feet as the smaller ones waddled off under the trees.

"Oh! That is so sweet! Are you angry?" Celina stepped closer, giggling. "It's okay. I won't hurt you. I just want to send your picture to Italy. You'll be world famous!"

The creature turned and lifted its tail.

Celina was admiring the fan of its lovely fluffy tail and snapping pictures when she found herself engulfed in an odor that caused her eyes to water and her stomach to heave.

Gagging and humiliated, Celina raced through the parking lot.

"What's that stink, Mommy?" asked a little girl standing with her family beside a grey BMW sedan.

"It smells like those cigarettes Ryan smokes on his balcony," replied her older brother.

Their dad looked up from the trunk of their car and wrinkled his nose. "That's skunk," he said. "Hurry and get in so the smell doesn't get in the car.'

Their mother hustled them into the back seat as she

added, "If Ryan ever offers to let you try one of those cigarettes, you tell him no. I don't want you living in our basement forever like that." She gave a littled shudder and muttered, "His poor mother," as she got into the front passenger seat.

Celina went around to the service entrance, uncertain what else to do. She had to check in for her shift, but surely she couldn't work in this state.

She had only just shut the door behind her when Daphne appeared at the end of the hallway, her nose twitching. She quickly wrapped the edge of her shirt across her nose. "Oh, Celina! Where did you find a skunk?"

Leeroy opened the service door, sniffed, and snickered, "I thought I smelled . . ." but then his face turned sickly green and he stepped back outside again.

Grace popped her head into the hallway from the lobby. "Daphne, there's an awful smell . . ." She looked at Celina and pointed out the door. "Out! Get outside now!" She pulled an N95 mask out of her pocket, and then a pair of latex gloves. "Celina, go to the old staff bunkhouse. I'll meet you there with the peroxide and baking soda. Before I get there, do not get wet! Water doesn't help!" She slammed the door behind Celina, who stood outside on the step and leaned her back against the door, wondering where the old staff bunkhouse was.

On the other side of the door she could hear Grace issuing commands. "Daphne, go find another uniform and some towels for her. I'll run to the kitchen. We'll meet back here, okay?"

Leeroy waved at Celina from the maintenance shed, fanning his nose and making faces at her.

Celina rolled her eyes. "Where's the bunkhouse?" she called.

Leeroy pointed to what looked like a larger old shed, though it did have a chimney and a row of small windows.

By the time she got there, Grace was coming out the door holding a big plastic bin of bottles, boxes, bowls, uniform, and towels.

She met Celina at the bunkhouse door with a pitying expression. "We'll have you cleaned up as much as possible, but skunk does linger, I'm afraid. I'm going to mix dish soap, this bottle of peroxide, and this baking soda into these bowls. Your job is to go into the shower stall and slather your dry self with it head to toe. Don't turn the water on! Let the paste sit a few minutes to work. Rub it into your hair and all over your body. Just don't get it in your eyes. After a bit, then you can rinse. You'll probably have to do it a couple of times. Use it all up. Then you can use this shampoo and body wash. While you're steeping, I'll soak your clothes in this other bowl. We may not be able to save them, but I'll try. When you're done, here's a clean uniform for you to wear."

Celina just blinked at her.

Grace handed her the foaming bowl of soap, soda, and peroxide and Celina stepped into the shower stall.

A couple of hours and a good deal of soap later, Celina nursed a hot tea in a clean Lodge uniform at the small table by the Lodge kitchen.

To her dismay, she saw Molly waving to her from outside

the restaurant, clearly intent on coming in and saying hello.

Celina burned with embarrassment. She sniffed the air around her suspiciously, wondering if she still smelled. Skunks were such cute beasts, but they were definitely trouble. She wasn't sure how she was going to tell this story to Giulia or to her family. Perhaps she wouldn't say anything.

"Hello, dear. How are you?"

"You probably don't want to sit there. I am sure I still smell like skunk," Celina said, colour rising in her cheeks.

"Oh, I think I can handle it, dear. Besides, I think Grace has something for you."

As if on cue, Grace walked into the dining room. She dropped a pile of clothes on the table. "I'm afraid this is all we have right now." In addition to a lumpy, oversized coat and some surprisingly new boots, Grace held up sweatpants with 'Bride Squad' written across the seat and a hoodie that read 'Old enough to know better. Too old to care.' "These will get you home at least."

Molly looked at the pile. "What about a hat?"

"This was the only one," Grace responded, displaying a green mesh baseball cap with a grain elevator logo.

Molly sniffed. "Well, that won't do. She needs something warm that hugs her head." She looked at Celina, who was sipping her tea and feeling incredibly thankful no one in Italy would ever see her in these clothes.

"Do you see how my hat is?" Molly added.

Celina nodded. "Yes. I like your hat. It's very nice. Is it a beanie hat?"

"We call them toques in Canada," said Daphne, looking

thoughtfully at Molly.

Suddenly, Molly's eyes lit up. "I have a stock of hats I've made for the craft fair. They're all different. There's sure to be one that suits you. Come and pick one for yourself. My gift to you."

19.
Wink and nudge

Molly O'Shea

Molly grasped the handrail to the creaky wooden steps that lead up to the grand, yet worn, doorway of the Laurel Lake Lodge. Molly had always loved the open veranda to the Lodge. She remembered how her parents had thought it was a risky venture for the Laurels, but even as a little girl Molly had thought Duke's parents were visionaries to build such a place in the middle of the mountains in front of the picturesque lake.

It had been quite run down, but it was returning to itself.

The wind had picked up since she'd left home and ventured around the lake to the Lodge. The dried cattails along the shoreline bent in the wind, and a skiff of snow whipped across the partially frozen lake and brushed against her face the entire way.

If the creaky steps and verandah floorboards were not enough to announce her arrival, the ring of the small brass bell that hung just inside the door frame should have brought someone to the front desk to greet her.

But no one came. She heard conversation near the back of the Lodge, near the kitchen, but she couldn't make out the words. Molly took off her brightly coloured crocheted tam and gloves, and brushed the snow from her eyelashes. Her rosy cheeks were even brighter from the cold wind, and her curly white hair looked like it had been through a bit of a storm. Molly chuckled as she caught a glimpse of herself in the oval mirror which hung over the foyer table. "I do look like a bit of a winter faerie today, don't I?" she said out loud to herself.

There was a cough that brought her back to herself. "Good morning, Miss O'Shea. How are you on this crisp morning?" Daphne asked.

"Daphne, my dear! Good morning!" Molly grinned up at her. "It is a crisp morning indeed, but I am doing splendidly this morning. And you? How are you today? How are you making on, while your father is so unwell? I trust that his health is improving? You are such a dear for being here. Such a big change for you, I'm sure. You'll have this place in top-notch shape again in no time."

Daphne paused just a little too long, and smiled. "I'm doing well, Miss O'Shea. Busy, of course, but I am managing. As for my father, he is recovering. He's home now, but he's staying mostly in his suite."

"Ms. Laurel. Can you come to the kitchen for a moment please?" a voice called from the kitchen.

Daphne turned her head toward the kitchen. "I'll be there in a moment." Daphne turned back to Molly.

"Good gracious, Daphne," Molly clucked. "Look at me prattling on like an old hen. What was I thinking? You have a place to run, and here I am talking your ear off. I was hoping to have some tea and scones this morning. Do you have any left? And if it is possible, I would love to sit at a table with a view over the lake."

"I believe there are still some scones in the kitchen, and I can put the kettle on for your tea in a moment." Daphne replied. "Please, follow me into the dining room. I think I have the perfect table for you."

Molly followed Daphne into the bright, sunlit dining room. The room had the comfortable smells of old wood, toast, and bacon and eggs. The amber-coloured hardwood floors creaked in spots as they walked across the room, but that was part of the charm of the old place. Sunlight streamed across the room, catching specks of dust that seemed to sparkle.

"Here you are Miss O'Shea", Daphne gestured to a small round table and two chairs. "Will this table do? I can almost see your house across the lake."

Molly's eyes sparkled as she glanced out the window. "It's an absolutely perfect spot, Daphne dear. I couldn't have chosen a better one myself."

Daphne pulled the chair out for Molly to sit down.

Molly looked up at Daphne once she had settled into the chair. "You are such a kind soul, Daphne. It's so sweet of you taking the time to look after an old hen like me, when you have all sorts of important things to do. Now, if it's not too much trouble, could I please have a spot of . . ."

"Irish breakfast tea?" Daphne finished Molly's sentence, grinning down at her. "Of course, I'll put the kettle on as soon as I'm back in the kitchen."

"Splendid!" Molly chirped. "And a scone or two if there are any left?" She hoped they weren't the rock hard specimens that new girl had been making. Maybe she should get a muffin, instead?

"I'm sure there's at least one warm scone in the kitchen with your name on it." Daphne winked.

Molly's smile grew even larger. "Such a dear! Now, one last request, if it's possible, and if it's not that's quite all right, then I'll get out of your hair."

Daphne looked at Molly's happy, rosy face. "May I guess, Miss O'Shea? Would you like a small dish of orange marmalade to go with your scones?"

Molly burst out laughing, and kept laughing until tears filled her eyes. Daphne couldn't help but laugh too.

Their laughter filled the dining room, and poured down the hallway toward the kitchen and customers rooms. Everything seemed lighter for a moment. Celina peeked from the kitchen to see what the laughter was all about.

"Oh, gracious me," Molly laughed and wiped away her tears. "Am I really that predictable?"

"Well," Daphne smiled and replied, "Yes, you are, but that's part of what we love."

"Thank you, Daphne. You are such a good girl."

"Thank you, Miss O'Shea. I'll be back in a moment with your tea, scones, and marmalade." Daphne headed toward the kitchen to prepare Molly's order. She turned around for a moment to see Miss O'Shea still chuckling and dabbing her tears away.

When Daphne returned to the dining room with the tray of scones, marmalade, and tea, Molly was no longer alone at her table. It was of their young guests seated with her—Leo, the tall, lanky man who'd been hovering silently around the

Lodge since he'd checked in. He seldom spoke except to say "Please" and "Thank you," but he had a kind face, though his eyes were sad.

As Daphne came up to the table, Leo glanced up, startled.

Molly was smiling, though. "Leo was just saying that he thought he might stick around Laurel Lake." She coughed into her handkerchief, and Daphne's eyebrows lowered. "Are you okay, Miss O'Shea?" Daphne asked.

Molly waved her hand. "Yes, dear. I'm fine. Just part of getting old."

Daphne and Leo exchanged looks.

Molly continued, "Leo needs a place to stay that's more long term. I just offered him my guest room. I hope you don't mind losing a paying guest."

Leo looked apologetically at Daphne. "I like the Lodge very much, but funds are low."

Daphne shrugged. "If Molly has room, that sounds like a good arrangement."

Molly nodded enthusiastically. "Oh, indeed. The room has a private entrance and its own bathroom. It will be much better for a young man to feel more settled. Not that the Lodge isn't perfectly lovely, Daphne."

Leo reached across the table and put his hand out to shake Molly's. "I'll pay a fair rate, of course."

She patted his hand. "Of course. We'll work something out. Perhaps you can do some chores around the place or something."

"Thank you," he whispered. "You have no idea what this

means to me."

Molly nodded. "You're welcome, dear. I must say, though, that I feel like I'm the one who's going to benefit, considering your good cooking."

Daphne eyed him. "Cooking?"

Leo blushed. "It's nothing." He turned to Molly, "When would you like me to move in?"

"Anytime, dear. You can come tonight if you'd like."

Leo grinned wider than he had in months. "I'll just go get my suitcase, then."

20.
Great ideas

Celina

Celina was kneeling in front of a large trunk in Molly's sitting room. The trunk, which also provided seating in the sunny front room, was filled with things Molly had knit or crocheted, including a dozen or more toques. There were amazing smells coming from Molly's kitchen.

As Celina poked through, examining the different hats, Molly asked with an obvious casualness, "How are things getting on in the Lodge kitchen, my dear?"

"Better, I think," said Celina, considering a green toque covered in crocheted flowers. "I think my muffins are okay now, but my scones are still not very good, I'm afraid."

Even though the menu had been simplified and even though her baking was somewhat improved, Celina knew perfectly well that it wasn't good enough. "Daphne said that there are more bookings next week, and we need to have hot breakfast again. I don't think I can do it. I can barely manage scorched scrambled eggs."

Molly pulled out a pair of mitts that matched the flower-covered hat and set them on the edge of the trunk. "Well, you're in luck, because I just happen to have some very tasty scones in my house today." She looked toward her kitchen and called out, "Leo, could you bring us tea and scones?" She leaned across the trunk and whispered to Celina with sparkling eyes, "It's like I have a personal butler!"

Celina laughed. She put on the green floral toque and the matching mittens and studied her ghostly reflection in the window. "I would like to take these. How much do I owe you?"

Molly waved her hand. "They're a gift." Her eyes twinkled again and she added, "Would you like me to add a little skunk face among the flowers to commemorate your encounter?"

Celina gave a little shudder. "No, thank you."

They were laughing on the couch when Leo came in holding a laden tray.

Celina helped herself to one of the scones on the tray, adding butter and preserves at Molly's urging. After her first tentative bite, Celina's eyes lit up, then she closed them and leaned back into the couch.

Molly chuckled. "Not quite what you expected?"

Celina shook her head, mouth too full to answer. She swallowed and said, "Mine are nothing like this. Mine are terrible! Like doughy stones!" She formed a fist, to demonstrate their density.

"Yes, well," Molly laughed. "Leo here is quite the baker. It turns out he's a professionally trained chef, in fact." Molly smiled warmly at the young man who still had not said a word. "He's got a stew going for my dinner."

Celina was still absorbed in the scone. "How do you do this?" The scones were light, buttery, and incredibly delicious.

"It's a matter of not overworking the dough and having a hot oven," Leo mumbled.

Molly looked over at Celina, "Maybe Leo can help you learn a thing or two in the kitchen."

Celina shook her head, "I would be better off if Leo just came and cooked at the Lodge. I was hired as a server, not a cook." She took another bite of the heavenly scone and then she blinked. "Leo! You're a trained chef! You have to come work at the Lodge!"

"I don't know about that," he said, backing up slightly and looking around.

Celina imagined no longer worrying about setting off the smoke alarm or killing a guest with raw pancakes. Leo could bake these heavenly scones for breakfast. "Leo, do you by any chance know how to make raspberry cordial?"

He looked over to Molly, who shrugged.

"I don't know," he said, "but I suppose I could look it up."

"Please say you'll come work at the Lodge!" she beamed at him.

"Why would Daphne hire me?"

Celina just gaped at him. She looked over at Molly. "Because as Molly could tell you, right now poor Daphne just has me for the breakfasts, and I'm awful. You tasted my scones, didn't you?"

Leo grimaced before he could mask his reaction and Celina laughed.

"Grace's mom has been coming in for an hour or two to make sandwiches for the cooler so there's something for the guests, but the Lodge needs to have hot meals, fresh food, and baking like this that tastes like heaven. Please go talk to her, Leo! I'm sure she'll hire you, especially with Molly's recommendation."

Molly nodded. "I can certainly give you a reference. Leo, you should take some food for her to try. She'll hire you on the spot."

"Perfect. That's settled then," said Celina before either Leo or Molly could back out.

And so, Leo set out with Celina to the Lodge, with a box containing a sample of Molly's dinner in his arms.

Celina sniffed at the box appreciatively, "That smells amazing."

Daphne was in the lobby speaking with a guest when they arrived. Christopher was behind the reception desk checking someone in.

Daphne glanced up as Celina waved at her and pointed to the dining room. Daphne excused herself from the guest and followed Celina and Leo into dining room. "What's up?"

Celina nodded to Leo. "I found you a chef."

"What?" Daphne turned and stared at Leo. "You stayed with us and bore our horrible food—sorry, Celina—and all this time you are a chef?"

"Yes, but . . ." He shrugged and looked away. "I wasn't looking for a job."

"Please tell me you're looking for one now?"

Celina went to the bussing station and grabbed a napkin roll of cutlery. She shooed Leo into the kitchen. "Go heat that up and show her."

"He's really a chef?" Daphne said to Celina as the

kitchen doors shut behind him.

"You should taste his scones."

Leo returned a few minutes later with a cloche on a tray.

He set the cloche and a plate of soda bread in front of Daphne. "It's nothing fancy, you understand. It's just what Molly asked me to make for her dinner, Irish stew with soda bread." He looked over at Celina. "If I'd known I was making a job application meal, I would have done something a bit more impressive."

He lifted the cloche and a delicious wave of flavourful scent rose up.

Daphne inhaled as she admired the gleaming broth, colourful vegetables, and meticulously diced meat. She took a tentative bite, closed her eyes to savour the flavours, and looked up at Leo, with wide eyes. "Mmmm," she murmured and took a bite of the soda bread.

Leo stood beside the table, hands behind his back, staring at the paintings on the dining room walls, waiting for her verdict.

Celina sat across the table, staring at Daphne, praying fervently that she would never have to cook in the Lodge kitchen again.

Finally, Daphne set down her fork. "Leo, this is incredible. The meat is so tender while the vegetables are firm. Everything is seasoned to perfection."

Celina looked between Leo and Daphne and thumped her hands on the table. "Please, Daphne, please. You know I can't cook like that. I won't be able to handle the breakfast rush. With Leo, the Lodge could actually be a popular dining place for locals and tourists."

Daphne smiled at her and stood to shake Leo's hand. "If you're willing, I'd love to have you join our staff."

Celina leaned back in her chair with a wide grin.

"What is that I smell?" Duke demanded as he poked his head around the entrance.

"We have a new chef," said Daphne. She indicated the remains of the meal in front of her.

"Do we? Don't I have some say about that?" Duke grabbed the spoon out from under the napkin and scooped some of the remaining stew. He chewed thoughtfully and then grunted.

Daphne quirked her brow at him. "Well? Do you approve?"

Duke shrugged. "I've tasted worse," he said.

21.
Cello translation

Alistar

Alistar was listening to the wind whistling through the rafters. Sometimes the stronger winds turned that whistle into a howl.

Alistar sat in a chair under the light of his bedside table lamp. The neck of his cello rested against his shoulder while he embraced the bout against himself. He always did this when he was lost in thought, drawing comfort from the strength of the instrument.

Alistar stared blankly at the floor as he plucked the A string repeatedly. He envisioned the priceless painting being thrown in the trash. He'd studied all the landscapes in the dining room. He didn't think any were the painting in Mr. Portello's sketch, but they were all similar. Lake, trees, and mountains.

Alistars' heart raced as he contemplated how he was going to save the painting if he couldn't identify it.

He moved his cello into the ready position. His fingers slid down the frets to an A sharp. The tensioned horse hair on the bow made contact with the strings bellowing out the full vibrations of the note. Alistar's ears perked up at the sound as his fingers moved to the next position, gliding the bow across the strings, the cello singing the beautiful beginning of his master composition.

Between the notes, Alistar heard the footsteps of other guests pause in the hallway outside his room.

He was overwhelmed with the confidence that the master composition inspired by the painting could translate his message of love to everyone.

He just needed to find it.

Alistar felt his heartbeat speed up as his mood shifted to fear. He struck a dissonant tone and stopped playing abruptly. He set the cello in its case and lay down in bed.

What if he couldn't afford the price they wanted for the painting? The thought that he might need to steal the painting to protect it flooded his mind as he clicked off the table lamp for the night. Would obtaining the painting in such a way destroy its message?

- - - - -

A small child's thudding footsteps in the hall pulled Alistar out of dreamland.

The thought of some scrambled eggs and bacon motivated him to get out of bed. He retrieved his favourite blue and grey hoodie from his suitcase. Alistar chuckled, remembering all the off-tune notes when the temperature in Mr. Portello's house dropped. Mr. Portello had been a mentor, but he'd nurtured Alistar like he was his own son, including gifting this hoodie one cold winter day.

The door clicked shut behind him as Alistar entered the hallway. The smell of fresh baked pastries, scrambled eggs, bacon, and potatoes wafted into the lobby from the dining room.

Standing near the reception desk, studying guests as if she were studying for an exam, was the young woman who'd checked Alistar in. Daphne. He needed to talk to her about the painting.

"Good day, Daphne," Alistar said as he checked her name tag. "Can we talk?"

Daphne stopped her scanning to meet Alistar's gaze. "Yes, of course. This way." She motioned for him to enter a small room next to the reception desk.

She followed without closing the door.

The desk was organized with a well-kept bookshelf full of some of the classics behind it. A small hand-carved sculpture of dolphins sat on the corner of the desk.

"That was gifted to me by a local Indigenous artist. Quite something, isn't it?" Daphne said, motioning toward the sculpture.

"So much detail on something so small." Alistar shook his head. "That's amazing."

Daphne sat down behind the desk. "How may I help you?"

"I'm Alistar, Alistar Montgomery." He extended his hand.

Daphne shook with a firm grip. "Yes, I remember." She glanced out the door as a family came chattering past. "What do you need?"

Alistar leaned forward in his chair. "I need your help. There is a painting here created by the one and only Savario. This painting was originally created specifically to be translated to music, following his principles of Rococo variation, but it went missing before my mentor was able to

142

see it. Savario died and no one was sure where the painting was.

"It was his greatest wish to find the painting. I have been going through the Savario archives at the University of Calgary, and I believe the painting was created here, and I desperately hope it is still here." He leaned his body across the desk, pleading with his eyes. "That painting is the key to my cello composition. I have to find it so I can translate the painting."

Daphne raised a brow. "Translated like through synesthesia? Won't any painting do that if you have the condition?"

"No, no. Not synesthesia." He brushed his hand through his already tousled hair. "You don't understand. I need that specific painting. There is nothing like it and never will be again."

"We have a lot of paintings here. What does it look like?"

Alistar pulled the notebook from his pocket and opened it to Mr. Portello's sketch. "Here," he said, pushing the book across the desk.

"I can think of at least a dozen paintings in the Lodge that look like this. How are you going to recognize the specific one?"

"I believe I will feel it here." Alistar placed his hand above his heart.

"Mr. Montgomery . . ."

Alistar felt the tension rise up his spine and blurted, "I can pay!" He stared intently at Daphne, trying to convey how important this was. "If you have someone on staff who knows where all the paintings like this are, I can pay them for their time."

Daphne sighed.

There was a crash from the dining room and she turned, shifting as if to rise.

Alistar thumped his hand on the desk. "The world needs this. People need to hear his message! The music is in the art."

"What exactly are you going to do with it if you find the painting that has this Rocococo . . ."

"Rococo variation, ma'am."

"How is that even possible?" Daphne stood up.

Alistar interlocked his fingers, turning the ends of his fingers white. "It needs to be heard. People will want to experience this. I just need to see the painting so I can translate it."

Daphne stepped to the entrance to the office. "It's probably on display here somewhere. Talk to Grace, our head of housekeeping. You can arrange to look with her. If you find it, you can move the painting to a wall in your guestroom, so you can study it and then *translate* it in peace." She stepped out of the little office, heading to the dining room. She looked over her shoulder and added, "Remember, quiet time is ten o'clock. No playing after that."

Alistar bit his knuckles to keep from squealing.

22.
Blank spaces

Grace

The next day Grace took Alistar through the building. "We'll start at the top and work down. I presume you've already checked all the paintings in the dining room and lobby?"

"Yes. It's not there."

The elevator opened on the fourth floor attic space, and Daphne unlocked Duke's studio. "It's strange to be in here when Duke's not here." She passed a finger along a table and grimaced. "Looks like someone has neglected the dusting up here."

"Isn't that your job?" said Alistar, heading for a stack of canvases against the wall.

As he flipped through the first stack, Alistar observed, "These are really good. Who painted them?"

From another stack, Grace said, "I think they're mostly Duke's own work. Have you met him? He's Daphne's dad. He was studying to be a professional painter before his father had an accident and Duke had to come back and take over here. But there were a lot of artists who came here to paint back in the time before I was born. My mom worked here for years, and she was a teen-ager back then. She told me that she remembers Savario and the rest of the gang in the 1960s. They were quite a bunch. She said there was art everywhere in those days. Oh, here's something." She pulled a canvas out of the stack and held it up. "What do you think?"

Alistar studied it, then closed his eyes, searching his feelings like a Jedi, trying to find a connection. After a minute or two he shook his head. "No. I don't think so, but maybe set it over there."

Grace leaned the painting against the legs of Duke's drafting table.

As they went through the various stacks lining the walls, they came up with three other possibilities. None were signed.

Grace had found one she thought was a perfect match to the sketch in Alistar's notebook, but that one was clearly signed D Laurel in the corner. "What a shame," she said.

"Yes. It'd have been wonderful if that was it."

"No, I meant it's a shame that this painting is hidden up here. So many of these are excellent. They should be on display so more people can see them."

"Ah, I see what you mean," Alistar said, but his mind was clearly elsewhere.

"That's this room done. It'll be easier now. The guest rooms mostly have just one or two paintings, and they're easily visible on the walls."

Alistar went to a door but Grace stopped him.

"Not that one, there are guests there. They're due to check out at eleven o'clock though, so we can come back then. Start over here."

They quickly went through the guest rooms. In the three floors of rooms, they found four possible paintings that they brought with them.

"They don't feel right," said Alistar. "But they look right. If I can't tell, maybe my cello will know."

"Hmm," said Grace with a sideways glance. They'd been at it five hours. She'd earned a hundred dollars, so she wasn't going to call him crazy.

They left all eight paintings in Alistar's room.

"I could use a coffee," said Grace.

"Good idea," said Alistar, looking at the stack of mountain scenes arrayed in his room. "I just don't know."

They stepped out of the elevator and were crossing the lobby to the dining room when Alistar stopped. He put an arm out to stop Grace.

He stared at the blank section of wall. "Do you see that?"

Grace was sure Alistar was nuts. "The wall?"

"That lighter rectangle. Do you see it?"

Grace stepped back. She shifted to the left and to the right. "Oh, yeah. I see it."

"Doesn't it look like something was hanging here?"

Celina stepped out of the dining room. "There was."

"What?" Alistar was breathless.

Celina shrugged. "A particularly ugly painting of mountains and lakes. Whoever made that one was no Botticelli, I can tell you!"

Alistar was turning a funny colour. "Where is it?"

"We had to move it when they were working on the floors, remember Grace?"

"Oh, yeah. Leeroy put it somewhere. I know I've seen it."

23.
Badly needed

Alistar

"I know!" said Celina. "Come on, I will take you to the room now."

Alistar almost stepped on the back of Grace's shoes as they left the lobby and went down a hall that ran along the back of the housekeeping area. Utility carts lined the hall. There were shelves of cleaning supplies and linens for the Lodge. At the end of the hall was the service entrance with a closet for staff coats. In front were a stack of cushions.

"It was right behind the couch here."

Alistar looked at her. "There's no couch."

Grace waved at the stack of cushions. "A really tatty old couch that was beneath the painting. Leeroy brought it all in here when they were fixing the floors."

Alistar scanned the room. "But there's no couch." Alistar felt faint, he looked in the closet and around the cushions.. There was no painting.

"They must have hauled the sofa to the dump and taken the painting with it," said Celina. "That's a shame."

Alistar's vision became watery. "It can't be. It can't be gone."

"Check out back by the dumpsters. Perhaps they left things there for the waste disposal company to take. That way." Grace pointed out the door. "Turn left"

"Thank you, thank you. May you have all the love in this world." Alistar gave Grace and Celina a departing smile.

The sharp cold of the handle made Alistar inhale as he opened the door to the backside of the Lodge. Large dumpsters to the left of the door were filled with black garbage bags.

A garbage truck was rumbling up the road. Alistar couldn't believe his luck.

Two men jumped out of the truck and started throwing the bags into the back.

"Wait, wait, wait!" Alistar shouted as he waved his arms.

Both men turned in his direction.

"There is something in those dumpsters that I need. I need to get in there now."

The larger-set man with a beard and messy salt and pepper hair barely corralled by a well-worn hat stood up. "Look, bud, we don't have time for you to dumpster dive. We are on a tight schedule and we still have to get down the mountain."

"Please, sir. You have no idea how badly I need this."

"Bugger off, dude," barked the thinner man. He had a beard that matched his partner's.

The men turned back to the dumpster. Each grabbed another bag which caused the pile to tumble forward. The bags came to a rest at the bottom of the dumpster and Alistar jumped on the spot.

Sitting at the back of the dumpster partially emerged from the pile was the corner of a worn wooden frame.

"That's it!" Alistar exclaimed as he lunged toward the dumpster. "That painting!"

"Uh uh! You can't just jump in there. You don't know what could stick ya."

"You get it for him then," came a commanding tone. Daphne stepped forward. "Just let him have it, boys."

The men swallowed in perfect synchronization.

"Well," said one. "If you're asking, Daphne"

"That's Ms. Laurel, to you," she said, doing something with her eyes that neither garbage man could look away from.

"I'll just get in there and get it," said the other man.

"Please." Alistar interlocked his fingers in a beseeching gesture, but neither garbage man was looking at him.

One hopped into the dumpster and passed the painting to his colleague who held it out to Daphne. "Here you are, Ms. Laurel."

"Thank you," she said, passing the painting to Alistar and turning back to the Lodge

"We'd be happy to buy you a drink at the Roadkill Café," called one. "Any time."

"We're there most nights," said the other.

"I'm sure you are," said Daphne over her shoulder and continued walking back into the Lodge.

Alistar followed her, clutching the painting against his chest.

"They don't make them like that here anymore," sighed one of the garbage men.

"Nope," replied the other, as he reached for the last

black bag. "What a power house."

"Kinda scary," his friend replied as he climbed into the driver's seat.

24.
Riding in

Betsy Buchanon

The roar of the motorcycle faded as Betsy switched off the engine and removed her helmet. When it was running, her bike purred between her legs like a giant beast. It always surprised her when she turned it off and it became a machine again.

There was an aliveness to the ride that nothing else in life had given her—not drinking, not smoking, and not even sex. The only thing that came close to the same thrill was when she saved an animal's life at her veterinary practice. Now, that was a high she could live off of for days.

The spring snowstorm was already starting to fill the air with fat white flakes, and she knew that driving anywhere else on her motorcycle right now would be dangerous. She certainly couldn't ride the hour and a half back home in this weather. So, it had seemed like a good omen when she'd seen the sign for Laurel Lake Lodge on the main highway. She'd turned off and driven up a gently winding road, the lake and mountains a picturesque view in the distance.

When she arrived, she could see that the Lodge wasn't as new as she might have hoped, and the little town she'd passed didn't offer many services. But maybe the isolation would be good for her.

Since she hadn't planned on staying overnight anywhere, she didn't have any luggage to weigh her down. As she struggled to walk against the wind, she skidded and slipped a bit as she made her way up the front steps and onto the porch. She opened the front door, but saw that there wasn't anyone behind the reception desk. Guess they weren't expecting anyone in this storm either.

There was an old-fashioned bell on the reception desk, though. She gave it two sharp taps and she didn't have long to wait before a woman about her age hurried down the stairs. "Hello!" she said brightly, heading behind the reception desk. "I'm Daphne. Sorry about the cold welcome, but we didn't have anyone scheduled to check in this evening."

"Do you have an available room?" Betsy asked, suddenly wondering if she would be out of luck. She couldn't ride any farther, and it was unlikely a service like Uber or Lyft would drive out into the middle of nowhere to pick her up, especially during nasty weather like this.

"Yes, we do," Daphne said quickly, and Betsy breathed out a sigh of relief. "For one?"

"For one," she agreed. "Got caught in that storm coming in and can't go farther tonight."

"It's good you came here," Daphne told her. "It's not safe driving out in this."

The wind was already howling around the windows. Betsy shuddered. "Yes. Especially on a motorcycle." She signed the guest registry and tapped her credit card on the reader.

Daphne handed her a key and her receipt. "Up one flight and last room on the left."

"Thanks." Betsy's stomach rumbled, and she realized the last time she'd had a meal was at breakfast. She'd been so busy at work today that she'd completely forgotten to take a break. Then, as soon as she'd gone home and showered, she'd hopped onto her bike and started driving. "Is there somewhere I can grab a bite?"

Daphne nodded behind Betsy. "The dining room is over there. They'll be open for another hour."

"Thanks."

The dining room had dark lighting, a wall of landscape paintings, and red velvet curtains at the windows framing a glorious view of the lake. While obviously worn, things looked well-cared-for and clean.

There was one older man drinking at the bar, but other than him, the place seemed empty. But as soon as she came through the entrance, a young woman pushed through the swinging kitchen doors and hurried over.

"Can I help you?" she asked in a friendly manner, her Italian accent was refreshing so far from a big city.

"Table for one," Betsy said with a twinge. If she ate out, it was normally with friends or family—if she was alone, she generally ordered takeout.

"Would you be interested in tonight's special? It's shepherd's pie. It's been very popular."

Betsy nodded, "Yes, that sounds perfect."

"And to drink?"

"Um. How about a honey brown ale? It's been a day."

"Very good," said the server as she turned to go to the kitchen.

Betsy pondered that her doctor would probably tell her that a drink should be off the menu for her, well . . . screw him. She was going to live a little, whether he liked it or not.

- - - - -

When Betsy woke up the next morning, she glanced out the window and groaned. It was still snowing.

She immediately reached for her phone and checked the weather forecast, which was something she'd neglected to do yesterday. Apparently, the snow would be heavy in the morning, but clear up in the afternoon as the day warmed up. The above-freezing temperatures and sun would cause a ferocious melting, probably turning most of the roads to slush. Terrible conditions to ride in. However, by the day after tomorrow, the continued warmer weather would clear up the worst of it.

"Guess I'm stuck here for the next day." She glanced down at herself—she'd stripped out of her jeans and jacket, but she would feel positively gross if she had to wear her clothes for another whole day. "Maybe they have a gift shop."

But when she rolled out of bed and checked downstairs, she got an apologetic smile. "No gift shop," she was told. "Although that's in the plans for the future."

Betsy bit her lip to avoid saying that a future gift shop wasn't much help to her now. "Is there some way I can get a new outfit? I wasn't planning on being here for this long, but the weather . . ."

Daphne brightened up. "Tell you what? After you eat

some breakfast, let me get you a bathrobe to wear in your room. Leave your clothes outside your door, and we can launder them and return them to you in a couple hours."

It was a generous offer. "Thanks," she said. "That's very nice of you."

Daphne shook her head and smiled. "Don't mention it. Always happy to find solutions for our guests."

"Okay, I'll be back here after breakfast to grab that robe."

However, after she returned to the front desk, Daphne was nowhere to be seen. Not until Betsy heard a commotion at the front door. In came her hostess, lending her arm to an older man who seemed unsteady on his feet. He was grumbling something, and Daphne bent her head toward him, arguing with him.

"I can walk by myself!" the man said, but Daphne replied with a roll of her eyes, "Doctor's orders, Dad." Looked like it wasn't the first time she'd said it.

Aha. That would explain why Daphne had seemed a bit frazzled. If she was taking care of her ailing father while running the Lodge, she must be exhausted—both were full-time jobs. Betsy knew that all too well.

Daphne helped her father toward the reception desk, pausing for one second to tell Betsy, "I'll be right with you."

"Take your time," she replied. She didn't have to add that she understood family was a top priority.

Daphne continued on her way, opening a door just behind the desk and disappearing inside with her father. After a couple of minutes, she returned alone.

"A robe, right?" she asked. "Be right back."

She went through another door into a service hallway and was back in less than a minute with a neatly folded robe. "Here you go."

Betsy thanked her, then retreated to her room to change out of her clothes and leave them to be cleaned. She took a long, hot shower and then watched some TV in her room—nothing to write home about. As promised, in two hours there was a soft knock on the door, and a young woman from housekeeping handed over a freshly pressed stack of clothes.

Later that day, Betsy wandered down into the lobby. Daphne was typing on the computer at the reception desk, but she paused when she saw Betsy. "Anything else I can help you with?"

Betsy shook her head. "No, I'm just a bit restless. I didn't expect this extended stay here, so I'm not sure what to do with myself."

Daphne grinned. "Workaholic?" she guessed. "I totally get it. I always have to be on the move too."

Betsy chuckled. "Well, I'm sure this place gives you plenty to do." She paused and her voice softened. "And your father—it must be tough. I went through something similar with my own dad."

She didn't say that she'd been much younger. Her dad had just turned forty and she'd been a teenager at the time of his heart attack. While it hadn't killed him outright, it'd begun the slippery slope of severe health problems that led to his death a few years later.

"I'm sorry," Daphne said softly. "It's not easy. He had a

stroke a couple months back, and he's been recovering. But he's still stubborn as hell. Even though he needs to be doing physical therapy regularly, he's pretty resistant to most of it."

Shrugging, Betsy advised, "Just keep at it. He'll thank you in the long run."

Her mind flashed back to her own dad's recovery. She'd been too young to push him to do what he should have done to take better care of himself, and her mom had been too stunned by the situation to step up when she was needed. While Betsy loved her mom dearly, her father's loss was tremendous.

Her thoughts moved to her own doctor's appointment a few days ago. He'd called her with the results yesterday, and the prognosis hadn't been good.

"Look, Betsy," he'd told her. "You need to take the pills I'm prescribing."

Betsy enjoyed his candour on most occasions, but this time it stung.

He added, "Your blood pressure is through the roof. If you don't start the medication, it's likely that you will end up like your father did. A heart attack could be in your future, sooner rather than later."

Seeing Daphne's father helped through the lobby was a stark reminder of what could be in store for her. Yet, at the same time, she'd spent her whole life avoiding taking medications. She felt most of them were unnecessary. She was healthier than that. Medications were like a crutch. The body worked better without them.

So, the idea of taking a pill every day—for the rest of her

life—seemed overwhelming. She knew that if she got on these drugs, she'd never get off them. Ever.

Of course, if she didn't take the drugs, perhaps her life wouldn't be that long either.

Her job as a veterinarian didn't help her coping levels, she knew. While she loved animals, even the difficult ones, there was a lot of heartbreak involved in the profession too. She hated those times when she couldn't save Fluffy or Muffin or Oscar and had to administer the final shot. It gutted her when she had to comfort the humans in her office as they lost a beloved family member. Those were times she could swear she felt her blood pressure go through the roof. She didn't need her doctor telling her it was so.

"If you're bored," Daphne interrupted her somber thoughts, "just stick around in the lobby for another half hour. A guest will play a cello composition inspired by a painting created here in the Lodge. It should be a show-stopping number."

Betsy perked up. "That could be great. Thanks."

- - - - -

The half hour seemed to drag by, but the performer was down in the lobby ten minutes before the show to set up beneath an old painting that seemed to be a view of the lake and mountains as viewed from the Lodge.

Was that the inspiration for the composition? Betsy thought the painting was hideous, but who was she to question taste? Her knowledge of artwork was about as large as her collection of teddy bears. Nonexistent. And that probably wasn't going to change anytime soon.

Music, though, was something she enjoyed. Especially classical music. It had been years since she'd been to a live performance, though. Usually, she was either too busy with work or too busy riding her bike. She didn't make time for anything else.

Well, the storm had forced time onto her. And through coincidence, it had brought her here to this live musical performance.

The performer took his cello from its case and settled on the chair. He looked around at the small gathering. A few people had phones out, plainly intending to capture the moment. A woman with a notebook in a pocket and a digital camera around her neck looked like a local reporter.

"Hi, everyone," he said.

The crowd settled down.

"Thank you, Daphne Laurel, for letting me set up here in this beautiful lodge." He paused dramatically, and Betsy glanced around. People smiled at one another. "I'm honoured that so many of you have come this snowy day to hear me play."

He drew the bow across a string and tweaked the tuning. "I'm Alistar Montgomery. I play cello professionally. This is a very special day for me. My mentor and good friend Mr. Portello told me about this painting years ago." He paused to give the audience time to study the painting as he tuned.

"I am so thankful to have finally found this culturally significant painting . . ."

"And rescuing it from the dumpster!" called out Grace.

Alistar nodded toward Daphne, "Thanks to Daphne, who has remarkable powers of persuasion. Without her I may not have been able to rescue it from the garbage men!"

The crowd laughed, as Celina, Grace, and Alistar exchanged knowing looks.

Alistar cleared his throat. "As I was saying, this is a significant painting that I've been searching for since my mentor first mentioned it. My search came to an end this week, and I was able to complete my master cello composition that would not have been possible without the inspiration of this incomparable painting by the great Savario. Without further ado, please enjoy my master compilation entitled, 'The Music In The Art.'"

Alistar bent over his instrument, and his bow caressed the strings. What emerged was a scattering of notes, both light and dark, that led the listener on a journey deep into the landscape. Betsy fell into the magical trip, carried on the music. She closed her eyes to better listen, her head tilted to catch the nuance of each sweet note.

However long it lasted, the music was over too soon. She blinked open her eyes, feeling empty without the song buoying her spirit. Like the others, she clapped and whistled her approval,

The man bowed his head solemnly to accept their praise. "Thank you for listening," he said, before setting the cello into its case.

People shook his hand or nodded as they began to drift away into the dining room, up to their rooms, or out through the doors.

Not her. Betsy marched up to him and introduced herself.

"Betsy," she said. "I just want to shake your hand."

"Alistar," he replied, taking her hand and giving it a firm shake.

"I have to admit that I wasn't impressed by that painting." She gestured behind him, and his beaming smile turned down slightly into a frown, as if she had insulted him personally. "But I was enraptured by your music. You, sir, are a virtuoso."

The compliment appeared to mollify him. "Thank you, thank you. I couldn't have done it without this marvelous painting, this incomparable artwork. Anything less would not have inspired the depths of my musical emotion." He placed a hand over his heart and bowed his head dramatically.

She nodded. "I'd love to talk to you more about your music," she said. "How about I buy you a drink?"

Alistar grinned. "I'd say: I never say no to a drink."

One drink led to two, and then three, over the course of the next few hours.

Alistar had a fascinating background, and the two of them seemed to get along like a house on fire. Before she knew it, the conversation turned away from Alistar's music and on to her.

"Why so glum?" he asked her, taking a sip of his beer. He seemed to savour each mouthful of the microbrew like a connoisseur.

She tried to brush him off, but he was persistent. Finally, she admitted about her medical history and the choice she had to face.

"But not really a choice at all, is it?" he asked. "One way you live; one way you die. The choice seems simple."

She shook her head stubbornly. "That's only a guess on my doctor's part. It's likely I might live for years longer with nothing happening. Or I could kick the bucket tomorrow. I don't know what I'm going to do, to be honest."

Alistar rubbed his chin. "The best advice I could give you is to live your life to the fullest. And to do so, you've got to actually live. You won't do that if you drop dead."

"I suppose," she muttered into her glass. "But who wants to admit that?" She would have to change a habit of a lifetime in order to have a lifetime to live. It was a little mind-boggling, to say the least.

At the last beer, Alistar began to talk about art—specifically, the painting that had inspired him. "I didn't want to talk about this publicly, for its safety, but this is a one-of-a-kind Savario," he told her.

"Really?" she asked skeptically. Even she had heard of Savario. Who hadn't? His work hung in every major museum. "Wow. An undiscovered piece by him would be worth a fortune!"

He nodded. "Exactly."

"Why do you think Savario left this painting here? And, the most important question, why do you have it now?"

He shook his head. "I don't. The muse has spoken through me today and I have nothing left to give. The painting is not mine. It belongs to the Lodge."

Wow. Lucky lodge owners. If Alistar was correct about its

value, they stood to make a fortune if they sold it.

- - - - -

The weather forecast was unfortunately accurate.

While the roads had been slushy the first day the snow started to melt, by the time day two rolled around, the melt had accelerated. The roads might be wet, but they wouldn't be too hazardous to take her motorcycle on.

"Thank you again for everything," she told Daphne as she handed over her room key at the front desk.

"My pleasure," Daphne beamed at her. Betsy thought she seemed different, lighter, perhaps, as if a large weight had been lifted from her shoulders.

The elevator door opened and Alistar came out, carrying his cello case. Behind him trailed Christopher carrying a music stand and a tote bag filled with papers.

"The hero of the hour!" Daphne exclaimed, throwing out her hands. She stepped out from behind the desk and reached to shake his free left hand. "You'll never know what a huge thing you've done for us. For this lodge. For all the employees here."

"Oh? How's that?"

"We sent an art appraiser pictures of the Savario, and he is flying in to see in. He estimated that if it's authenticated, it could make hundreds of thousands at auction. We'll be able to afford improvements to the Lodge. We can't thank you enough."

"I confess, I'll be sad that it won't be here to admire when I come back."

"We'll have prints made," Daphne said. "We can sell

those, too. And include the link to your music download so everyone can enjoy your composition."

Alistar perked his head back up. "You're so kind."

"And you're pretty awesome."

"He is pretty great, isn't he?" said Betsy, smiling up at Alistar. "He's been a help to everyone around at the Lodge, me included."

He grinned down at her. "Decided a little pharmaceutical help was okay?

Betsy nodded. She'd spent all night thinking about what he said and she had made her decision.

If she had no problem prescribing medications every day to cats and dogs to make their lives better, why couldn't she take pills to help herself? How was she any different from them?

She wasn't, of course. If medication would help her live a long and full life, then she should take it. She trusted her doctor, didn't she? So, she should trust him in this too.

Laurel Lake was a special place, she'd realized. Not just because of people like Alistar, who gave her a wave as he headed out the door. And not just because of staff like Daphne, who went the extra mile to make guests feel comfortable and at home. Not even for the wonderful food Celina and Leo served at the restaurant or the beautiful vista out the windows.

No, beyond all those aspects, Laurel Lake Lodge had a sense of peace to it. She had desperately needed that peace.

Each time she rode away from her problems on her

motorcycle, they just followed her back home again.

What she'd needed were answers. She'd found them here. Answers that she'd spent a long time looking for in all the wrong places.

This was a special place, and others could be helped by it, too. She couldn't keep it a secret. She wanted to return here again as soon as she could, and she could hardly wait to bring her friends, especially her group of biker ladies, who might not fit in everywhere—like her—but would be welcomed here with open arms.

25.
Back again

Yize

Several months after Yize Peng's first visit to the Lodge, he had become a regular. He was welcomed by staff and the other visitors alike. He guided his tour bus of visitors through the Lodge's many original features, relayed the history of the area, and led hikes around the lake and beyond.

Laurel Lake Lodge had become a popular destination in the Canada Far & Wide portfolio, part of their popular mountain tour of Waterton, Laurel Lake, Banff, the Icefield Parkway, and finally Jasper. The tour guests usually only stayed overnight, but the stunning location made an impact and they filled social media with images of breathtaking vistas. People who saw their posts were starting to book stays.

There was still work to do to make the Lodge more luxurious, but its unique charm and setting, coupled with the opportunity for numerous hiking trail excursions, ensured repeat bookings.

As he parked the tour van in front of the Lodge, he noticed the parking lot was quite full. There was even a motorcycle. So many vehicles attested to the improvements Daphne had been making.

A woman stood next to the impressive motorcycle with

Leeroy Lemon. They each held up a hand in greeting when they saw him.

Yize got the group of twelve out of the van and showed the way to the bathrooms and dining room, where Chef would have a buffet set out for them. Then returning to the van to gather his case of promotional materials and his hiking gear, he approached the pair.

"Good morning, Leeroy. Looks like a perfect day for a hike."

"Hey, Yize," Leeroy nodded. "Yup. Ideal weather." He waved an arm to indicate the woman who was dressed in leathers. "Do you know Betsy Buchanon? She is a visitor and has some questions about the Lodge. I was just telling her that you're a good one to talk to."

Yize shook the woman's hand, with a quizzical glance at Leeroy who'd grown up at Laurel Lake and certainly would be able to answer any questions a tourist came up with.

Leeroy just smirked at him. "I'll just leave you to it, eh?" He patted his chest pocket. "I've still got things on the list. See you around."

Yize and Betsy headed up the porch stairs. Yize was pleased to see they seemed much sturdier than they'd been at his last visit.

In the dining room he checked that his tour group were all doing fine and then joined her at a table off to the side.

When Christopher came up to them, Yize asked Betsy, "Can I get you a coffee?"

"That would be great, thanks." She looked up at Christopher and asked, "How are those scones I saw in the cabinet?"

"So much better than they used to be," he said with a wink to Yize. "The new chef is a fantastic baker. We also have wonderful local jam to go with them. Shall I heat a scone up for you?"

"That sounds great." She watched Christopher head off for their coffees and said, "That young man has an old soul."

Yize nodded. "He does. If you come back here, I think you'll find there are a lot of old souls among the regulars. It's something to do with the magic of the place, I think."

"Can you tell me what you know about that? And its history?" She glanced over to the tour group and added, "If you have time, that is."

"Of course. Until the group finishes their lunch, I'm at your disposal."

Christopher set down their coffees, a bowl of small containers of cream on ice, and a bowl of sugar packets. "I'll be right back with your scone."

Yize pushed the bowls toward Betsy. "Do you want cream and sugar?"

"Just cream for me, thank you."

"What do you want to know first, Ms. Buchanan?"

"Oh, please call me Betsy." She sipped her coffee and looked out at the lake. "Well, how about you start with what you know of this history?"

As they drank their coffee, Yize relayed everything he knew about the Lodge and its past and present owners. He gave Betsy one of the promotional brochures. "You see we arrange some interesting tours in the region, several of which stop here at Laurel Lake. I would be delighted if you'd be kind enough to mention them to family and friends."

"I have to say, Yize, your enthusiasm and obvious knowledge has given me more information than I was expecting. I've travelled all over, but rarely heard such a thorough presentation."

"Thank you," Yize smiled at her. "I pride myself on in-depth research."

Betsy added, "I'll be bringing friends here for certain. I am a member of a motorcycle club and we are always looking for new routes and destinations. Have you ever considered putting together a motorcycle tour?"

"Huh. No, but that's an interesting idea. Maybe we could look at some routes around the surrounding area that would be perfect for riding?"

Betsy grinned. "Let me give you my number. My club has a meeting next week, so we will definitely talk about this. Give me a call and we can organize something that benefits us both."

Yize saw that his group had finished their desserts and were beginning to look restless. He stood up and put out his hand to shake hers. "It's been a pleasure to meet you, Betsy. I look forward to touring with you."

"Ditto."

Yize walked to the lobby smiling. He restocked the leaflet holder. As he escorted the group out to start their walk around the lake, he was glad that he'd made a new contact. With Betsy's help he could make the Lodge an even better venue for his clients and expand his outreach to other motorcycle touring clubs.

26.
Being Savage

Darren Jr.
(who still identifies as Clint)

Darren Laurel Jr. had pocketed the tuition money and funds his father had given him for his first year at business school and headed out to seek his fortune.

From the day of Darren Jr.'s birth, Duke had been grooming his son to take over the Lodge and continue the family tradition. Daphne was older, but Duke said women didn't have what it took to run a place like Laurel Lake Lodge. Women, he claimed, were irresponsible.

Darren Jr. had the gift of the gab—an outgoing, dynamic personality. During his teens, Duke told everyone that Darren Jr. was a natural, because he was so much better suited to dealing with guests than Duke was. Guest relations were definitely not Duke's strong suit. Duke said all Darren Jr. needed was some understandings of the business end of things, and the future of the Lodge would be assured. The family business would continue. Duke told Darren he'd slowly turn over the reins of the Lodge to him once he had his degree. Then Duke planned to return to his true passion, his art.

But Darren Jr. had had very little interest in Duke's plans

for him. He'd evade any chores assigned to him, disappearing off into the forest with his friend Leeroy Lemon, and they wouldn't return until dark when the wolves started howling high in the passes.

One hot August day Darren and Leeroy had set the woods near the Lodge ablaze. The lodge was saved, but it was a very large straw that broke the metaphorical camel's back. Duke was done.

That September, Darren Jr. was shipped off to the St. Swithen's Academy boarding school where Duke claimed he would learn some discipline, become a man, and be rid of the undesirable traits which, Duke concluded, could only have come from his mother.

St. Swithen's Academy was a traditional institution based upon the English public school model. Headmaster J.T. Swackhammer proudly declared that the school was run on what he called 'The Seven C's: Conduct, Classics, Christianity, Cold Baths, Cricket, and Cleanliness.' The seventh C, Corporal Punishment, had been outlawed, but the masters and prefects had their ways of working around this short-sighted legality.

During his years at St. Swithen's, Darren Jr. attempted to forge bonds with sons of the elite. Limousines dropped his classmates off at the school's entrance while Darren Jr. walked over from the Greyhound station. His classmates spent Christmas in the British Virgin Islands, while Darren Jr. was snowbound at Laurel Lake Lodge. And in their latter years at the school, they'd head off for bacchanalian weekends in the city, while Darren Jr. spent his precious pocket money on bottles of warm beer from the local bootlegger, drinking them in the darkness beneath the rugby goal posts.

Occasionally, thanks to Darren's ability to talk a blue streak and his willingness to push the bounds of outrageousness, his classmates would take him under their wing. Darren was always good for a laugh, so they'd invite him along—an Easter skiing at Whistler, a May Long Weekend surfing in Tofino, or a week of carousing in Vancouver. After this taste for a life of Porsches, Gucci, and the Hilton, the idea of returning to Laurel Lake and running the family's lodge was anathema.

He'd decided back then that Laurel Lake Lodge was in his past, but now he considered the possibilities.

Blood's thicker than water. Blood's thicker than water. He repeated the phrase over and over in his mind as he drove his rental car from the Calgary Airport toward Laurel Lake. *The old man'll be glad to see me again. I'm sure of it. And with all that cash from the sale of the old lodge, he'll need investment advice. And what better place to invest than the Fountain of Youth Retirement Resort! I might even give him a family discount if he wants to move there.*

Pitching his retirement home venture to Eve of Destruction Resources may have been a Hail Mary, but offering a can't-miss investment to his own flesh and blood should be a slam dunk.

He hadn't hesitated a moment to max out his credit cards to make the trip to Laurel Lake.

When he pulled into the driveway of Laurel Lake Lodge,

a strange feeling of nostalgia washed over him. "Unbelievable. It hasn't changed one single bit," he mumbled.

When he parked the car and walked across the grounds, the years since he'd last been there dissolved with each step. "Incredible," he murmured, shaking his head. "It's like this place is frozen in time."

The old lodge still had those wonky old stairs, and the old sign over the front door was still so faded you could barely make out the lettering. The siding was still that unspecific colour that was probably once white but was now a mottled texture of peeling, cracking grey paint.

Clint looked over at the forest and, immediately, an image came back to him of Leeroy and him running for their lives after their campfire got away on them. With a chuckle he wondered about his stash. Was his dope still buried in that old coffee can in the woods? That was worth a look. He wasn't ready to face Duke quite yet.

He followed the path into the forest, scanning for that old charred stump where he'd hidden his precious can. But the forest had grown over the years, so he couldn't spot it right away. He left the trail, pushing bushes and low-hanging tree branches aside, thrashing his way in the general direction of his own version of buried treasure. Clint waved at clouds of mosquitos and fought his way through the dense undergrowth when he heard a voice.

"Have you lost something?"

Clint turned to see a guy standing back on the trail, waving his hands in front of his face and slapping the back of his neck.

"Ah . . . no, not really," Clint replied. "I'm just having a look around. The old haunts from when I was a kid." He abandoned his search for now and headed back to the trail.

"You used to live here as a kid?" the guy said.

"Yep. Me and twenty billion mosquitoes," Clint said, slapping his forehead.

"This must have been an amazing place to grow up . . . except for the mosquitoes, that is."

Clint slapped his neck, and said, "It didn't seem amazing at the time. But, yeah, I guess it was a pretty unique childhood."

The guy held out his hand and said, "Yize Peng. Nice to meet you."

"Clint Savage. So, what are you doing in Duke Laurel's idea of paradise?"

"You might say I'm a scout."

Clint did a double take. When Winky was talking about his boss, Clint hadn't visualized a little guy like this. He'd thought the boss's name was Scout, but this made more sense. They were scouting out the property.

"How about we head to where the bugs aren't so bad," Clint said, leading Yize out of the woods. "So, you're here to check out the Lodge for business purposes?"

"Yes. My company is very aggressive when it comes to finding new locations. This old lodge might not look like much, but I think there's a hidden value most people don't realize."

"I know exactly what you're getting at," Clint said, with a

knowing grin. "Most people look at a place like this and all they see are rocks, trees, water, and a crappy old lodge. But you and I know that the real value lies deeper."

"Oh, for sure," Yize said, and nodded enthusiastically. "That's what our company's all about. Finding hidden gems."

"Absolutely!" Darren slapped Yike on the back. "And I'm here to help you get exactly what you want. Know what I mean? I'm happy to give you some inside information that might be useful to you."

"Oh, well, yes. I'd appreciate any help you can give me. You've obviously got some local knowledge that could be a big help."

"Absolutely! Absolutely! Absolutely!" Clint continued to slap Yize on the back.

"Great. Well, for starters, this trail we're on . . . where does it take you?"

Clint figured Yize was probably interested in how they'd access the next property. Maybe it was about road access for when they opened a mine.

Darren looked up the trail, and said, "Well, the trail goes on pretty much forever. When we were kids, my buddy Leeroy and I, we'd pack some jam sandwiches and cartons of chocolate milk and follow the trail until the sun was just above that mountain over there. Yeah, we had all sorts of adventures out there in the bush. Then, we'd hustle home and get back in the dark. One time, we took a tent and our sleeping bags. We planned to stay out over night, but about midnight we heard a howling sound.

We figured it was a sasquatch. We jumped out of our

sleeping bags, and we couldn't find our flashlight, so we ran like crazy through the dark. And when we got back to the Lodge, we heard the same sound. It was the wind howling through the branches of the trees."

Clint snapped back to the present when Yize said, "Those sound like some great memories."

"Yeah," Clint said, ambling down the trail back toward the Lodge. "I'll show you a secret spot Leeroy and I had for fishing." Clint danced along the boulders that lined the lake with Yize stumbling behind.

"Here!" Clint shouted with excitement. "We used to stand on this boulder and cast into the lake. We'd spend hours out here. Didn't matter if we caught anything. We just loved being out here. On hot summer days, we'd climb up to those cliffs up over there and jump."

"Sounds terrifying," Yize said.

"Yeah, the first few times were pretty scary. But eventually, we got so we could do backflips." Clint paused, chuckled to himself, "Yeah, it was pretty wild."

"You're one lucky guy," Yize said.

Clint's eyes continued to scan the panorama. "Lucky? Me?"

"I grew up in a townhouse, and I wasn't allowed in our tiny back yard because my grandmother didn't want me to get dirty. To her, playing outside was a waste of time."

Yize wasn't sure Clint hadn't heard him. He stood silently on that boulder, looking out over the lake and the surrounding mountains, grinning.

Finally, Clint said, "I guess you're right. I never realized until now how . . ." Then, he turned to Yize, and his gaze transformed suddenly from peaceful to hostile. "So, what great plans does Eve of Destruction Resources have for this place to bring all the money in? First, clearcut the forest, then carve out your open pit mine? Fill the lake with sludge?"

"Eve of what?" Yize said, taking a step back.

Clint glared at him. "I know you represent Eve of Destruction Resources. I'm an old friend of Richard Smyth-Washburn. His real name's Winky, by the way. He told me all about your plans for this place. I know you want to the Lodge so you can add to the adjacent properties. Then, it won't be just the eve of destruction, it'll be the end . . ."

"Whoa! Hold on," Yize said, palms raised. "I'm definitely not from Eve of Destruction Resources, and I'm not here to buy the Lodge. I'm with Canada Far & Wide. We're a tour company. I scout out new locations to add to our roster of tours. A clearcut forest and an open pit mine wouldn't exactly be a tourist draw. My goal is to bring tourists here so they can fall in love with Laurel Lake Lodge just like you did."

Clint had never put the word "love" together with Laurel Lake Lodge, but Yize was right. He looked around him at the lake and mountains. He took a deep breath, inhaling the frest scent of the pines. "Huh," he said.

Beyond all his bad memories of his adolescent conflicts with Duke, he actually did love this place. Maybe this wasn't such an awful legacy after all.

Clint stepped toward Yize. "You're not here to destroy things?"

Yize shook his head.

Clint extended his hand, and said, "In that case, how about I reintroduce myself. My name is Darren Laurel, Junior. You probably know my father, Duke."

27.
The promise

Jonathan "Eddie" Edwards

Jonathan M Edwards sat in a leather-upholstered chesterfield chair in Room 306, staring out the balcony windows at the lake and forest around him, lost in thought. The room was compact, adorned with dated accessories that accented the walls. Classic, solid furniture pieces, including chairs, a table, and an elegant headboard occupied the chamber. Despite the charming setting, it implied management refrained from pursuing investments in renovations. He approved such fiscal responsibility.

Slithers of early morning sunlight wrestled with the elaborate pinched pleats of the curtains, breaking through to penetrate the somber atmosphere. Curtain tiebacks lay discarded next to the dusty and chipped baseboard. Fingers of light played with the design of the rug, teasing the artistic weaves and knots of the fading motif.

After Agnes's death, Jonathan Edwards had been trapped in a nightmare. Time seemed to have stopped for him as his life descended into pits of agonizing grief.

His passion for his research and his writing withered, atrophied, and molded.

His students had become faceless and lectures seemed pointless. His supervisor informed him it was time for retirement.

He'd been too exhausted to object.

Being retired had just hastened the suffocating grip of anguish and the excruciating weight of his despair.

Standing in the apartment they once shared he knew he had to get away. He needed to keep his promise to Agnes, so here he was.

The glow from his laptop monitor on the table outlined his broad shoulders. The lapel of his grey tailored suit sagged, the pants were baggy, and the hem slumped over the high-shine leather finish of his Oxfords. His pocket watch, suspended on a triple metal chain, was frozen at three forty-six. A pair of reading glasses dangled from the fingertips of one hand while in the other, a tumbler now containing only the vapours of Scotch whisky, stealthily drifted from his grip. Black suspenders draped over his wide chest and sharply clipped to the waistband of the trousers. His starched white shirt opened at the collar, the Windsor knot of his necktie was undone and hung lopsided around his neck.

The head of wavy brown hair was streaked with veins of silver. His face was clean-shaven except for a generous mustache. All other features became insignificant to his eyes; they were a dark coffee brown, moist with his pain.

He looked toward the bed, looking for Agnes, before he remembered that she was not there. Grief stabbed his heart yet again.

He sank deeper into the cushion of the chair. He let the tumbler drop to the rug. It landed with a muffled clunk but didn't break. He folded his reading glasses and tucked them into their holder in the outer breast pocket of the suit, behind the pocket square.

Before Agnes, he hadn't taken care of himself. He'd focused on his academic writing, honing his craft, finding his voice, pursuing his despairing quest for the elusive notable achievements. All other aspects of his existence diminished.

After Agnes, he had a regimen of regular exercise. He did not smoke, drink, or eat fast food. It was easy to do when it was for her. His writing flowed effortlessly. He planned to write a novel someday, and she believed he would.

If she were here now, the bed would be turned down, his clothes would be hanging meticulously in the closet and folded tidily in the drawers. The curtains would be drawn open to the full length of the rod to let in the sunlight and the fabric would be swaying in the breeze like sheets on a clothesline.

Instead, his luggage remained on the floor, abandoned where he'd dropped it when he checked in.

If she were there, she would say, "Smell the air. It's beautiful. Let's go for a walk around the lake." She would pull his arm, and he would concede. He always gave into anything she wanted and life was better for it. She knew what he needed.

He missed her voice.

At the end of their walk when they retired to their room, she'd fling herself on the bed, making the springs protest. Her laugh propelled him into new possibilities. When she pressed her lips to his with a hard, intense desire, he lost himself. He was adrift in her eyes, swept away with her scent and delirious to her touch. He was amazed how someone could love him, how anyone could love him, how she dared to love him. She emboldened him with the unimaginable journey to love itself. He missed her laugh, her midnight hair and alabaster complexion, but he still felt her love. And if he strained his ears, he was sure he could hear her laughter in the trees when he was here at Laurel Lake Lodge.

She'd been there when his first articles were published, when his pieces became long-listed, then short-listed, and when, beyond all the conceivable odds, he finally won awards. And then he won again and again. Literary agents called, publishers begged for more articles and books, bookstores pleaded for author readings, networks requested interviews, his university classes became more popular.

For all of it, Agnes was there. She stood at his side, acting as his support, his sustenance, the nourishment to his soul. She knew his secret dream to write a novel. She made him come to Laurel Lodge and write stories instead of academic treatises. She was the love of his life and she wanted his dreams to come true.

If she were here he would wake up to the whistle of a boiling kettle. But so often they were distracted by lovemaking and the water grew cold.

So much joy.

But then her headaches had started.

He recalled the scent of antiseptics, cleaning products, medical supplies, and human excreta escaping hospital doors.

He walked beside her when the hospital hallway stretched long, narrowing into an uncertain future, and until, at appointment after appointment, the sterile halls were as desolate as his fading hope.

Eventually, Aggie was in hospice care. Stoic and impassive, a nurse, brisk in her sparing words, had directed him to the room. "It's only a matter of time. She will not gain consciousness." The nurse checked the monitor attached to his beloved wife. Multi-coloured numbers, wavy lines, and neon signals flashed on and off.

Jonathan watched the nurse leave the room. He'd sat in a high back chair next to Agnes's hospital bed. He pressed his head on the aluminum bed rail. The metal bar left a cleft in his forehead. He thought the vertical side rails incarcerated her in that bed like she was behind the bars of a prison.

He willed her to open her eyes just once more.

As if she had heard his silent plea, her eyes fluttered open and her gaze fastened to his face. She squeezed his hand. Her grip was weak and trembling. "Eddie, promise me." As she held fast to his hand, he leaned closer. She kissed his face. "Finish that novel. Keep going. Visit our special place. Promise me."

He could not utter a single sound. His throat was constricted with despair and heartache. He swallowed his pain and it wedged next to his heart. He managed a nod and finally a hoarse whisper, "Yes, I promise."

She smiled. Her hand went limp and she closed her eyes. She exhaled a deep sigh. It was her last breath. He glanced up at the clock. It was three forty-six.

- - - - -

Outside his room, children's feet thudded down the corridor as they raced to the elevator.

Jonathan Edwards looked longingly to where Agnes should be curled up reading a book, waiting for him to finish his writing so they could go down to dinner. His stomach growled.

He blinked back his tears, and rose to find something to eat.

28.
Old times

Maxine

On her way through the lobby, Maxine glanced to the bar in the dining room. That was the only part of the Lodge business that had interested her when she lived here. She had always loved listening to patrons from all over the world sharing their quirky lives and telling about their dreams. Those stories had been a balm amid the drudgery of helping Duke manage this never-ending nightmare.

Far from the hopping scene she remembered fondly, there sat one lone, hunched-over patron—an older man swirling his glass at a small bar area squished between the kitchen door and the windows. He stared into his glass with intensity. The half-empty bottle of whisky near his glass called to Maxine. A drink is exactly what she needed.

"Mind if I join you?" she asked, setting her laptop on the bar stool between them. "It's been quite the day."

In slow motion, he turned to Maxine and blinked. "More like quite the month," he slurred, "Miserable is how I'd describe it. A miserable, miserable month. Definitely." He took a sip of his drink and set it down. "This is the only thing that makes it bearable."

He picked up the bottle and showed Maxine the label. "In case you're wondering, the bar's closed. I had to bring my own." He slid off his stool, shuffled behind the bar, and took a clean glass off the shelf. Standing behind the bar like a publican, he expertly poured a quarter measure, then topped up his own glass. "Hope you like it neat." He slid the glass to Maxine.

"Thank you." She took a sip and said, "I used to work here, a long time ago. You look familiar."

He shuffled back to his seat and looked blurrily at her. "Well. I could be. We've been coming here a long time." Tears welled in his eyes, and he turned his focus to his glass.

"Oh!" she said, as the vision of a younger man and his delightful wife formed in her mind. "Are you, Professor Edwards?"

He held up his glass as if to make a toast and said, "That I am. Call me Jonathan. Or Eddie. Just not Professor, if you don't mind."

Maxine's eyes brightened. "Wow! It's so wonderful to see you after all these years! I'm not sure if you remember me. I'm Maxine. I loved talking with you and your wife when I tended the bar." She looked at the six stools. "Of course, it was bigger then."

Jonathan squinted at her. She could almost see cogs whirling in his brain. Finally he said, "Yes, I do remember those eyes and that smile. Maxine. Of course. You were the wife."

Maxine raised her glass in a salute of acknowledgement. "I was."

"We often wondered what happened to you."

"Duke didn't say?"

His lip quirked. "Oh, no. If anyone mentioned your name, he glowered so furiously they didn't dare continue. But we wondered. I'm glad to see you looking so well." He raised his glass. "To your good health." He took a big swallow.

"I remember your lovely wife," she said hesitantly.

"I lost her thirty-two days ago." He looked away.

"I'm so sorry. You two were like magic together. I can't imagine how hard it must be for you." Back then, the perfect chemistry she saw between the Eddie and his wife was a painful contrast to her relationship with Duke. "She was Agnes, right?"

He nodded, blinking through tears. He reached into his jacket and pulled out a hankerchief to wipe his eyes and blow his nose.

"I've thought of her." Maxine paused, "Thought of both of you, really, many times since I left here. I always wanted to thank Agnes for her kindness, but you know how it is. Life got in the way every time I thought about tracking you down and reaching out." Maxine inhaled the woody caramel scent in her glass. "Excellent whisky, by the way." She took a swig and let the smoothness linger on her tongue then glide down her throat. "Would it be okay if I shared a story about your wife that means the world to me?"

Jonathan's eyes filled with tears. "I would very much like that, but please forgive me if I become emotional. I'm lost without her. I don't know how I'm supposed to keep living." He pointed to the bottle. "I know that this—is making things worse, but it's also the only thing that helps dull the pain.

"I'm sorry things are such a struggle." Maxine put a hand on his shoulder. If there's anything I can do, let me know."

"Hearing your story might help."

"All right. In the spring of 1983, Agnes found me falling apart at the gazebo during her morning walk around the lake. I think you were holed up in the room working on your latest writing project." Maxine took a sip and let the warmth soothe her throat and dull the pain of the memory. "Things had been rough for me since the birth of our son, Darren. I had started taking an antidepressant, but it seemed to make things worse. Suicidal thoughts bombarded my brain day and night. Agnes was so kind, I told her I couldn't take it anymore, and I shared my exit plans. She convinced me to go to the hospital. I didn't want to go to the Laurel Lake Hospital because the whole town would know. She said that was an easy problem to solve and she drove me into the city. She told me I deserved to be happy. I don't think anyone had ever said that to me before."

Jonathan nodded. "Yes. I remember Agnes telling me how worried she was about you. When we didn't see you the next year, we were afraid of the worst. Agnes asked the housekeeper, but she just said you were gone, and not to mention you around Duke. "I'm glad to see you looking healthy and well after all these years. I hope that after you left, your struggles ended quickly."

"They did. I was lucky. I switched medications and never looked back."

Professor Edwards smiled. "My Agnes was pretty good at convincing people to do what they needed."

Maxine nodded in agreement. "She helped me see my future beyond Laurel Lake. Between that idea and the new medicine, I had the strength to break free from the prison of my marriage." Maxine's voice began to shake. "I wasn't as lucky as she was when she found you." She looked into Professor Edward's eyes and a tear rolled down her cheek. "Agnes is the reason I'm alive." Maxine downed the rest of her drink. "And because I'm alive and fighting, so far thirteen wrongly incarcerated prisoners have been set free. Agnes made a difference in the world."

She stood up and put her hand on Jonathan's shoulder. "I'd like to honour her by helping you the way she helped me. Jonathan Edwards, you deserve to be happy."

Jonathan rested his elbows on the bar and put his head in his hands. "How can I be happy without Aggie?"

"Can I take you to a doctor or the hospital and get some help? We could go right now." She looked at the glasses. "We'll call a taxi."

Jonathan shook his head. "I can't go anywhere now, I'm a mess," he choked out.

"Fair enough. It's probably better to be sober. How about we go after breakfast tomorrow morning?"

Jonathan nodded, lips quivering. "I think Aggie would like that."

"Me, too."

29.
A letter

Maxine

When she got to her room, Maxine found a wrinkled envelope leaning against the lamp on the desk. She picked it up and studied three bold black uppercase letters: MOM. She assumed it was the Lodge paperwork Daphne had said they'd do later. She could fill it out after a long hot shower.

Refreshed and more relaxed, she propped the lumpy pillows up against the headboard and climbed under the flimsy covers. The lodge needed to get some five-star worthy duvets.

The envelope had dirty smudges and a musty odor that made her hesitate. Why did everything at Laurel Lake seem like it past its prime? Everything seemed worn and outdated. After the last couple of days, she was beginning to feel the same way about herself.

When she took them out of the envelope, the papers weren't her registration receipts. Rather, they were pages torn from a Laurel Lake Lodge notepad, in the distinctive handwriting she recognized from his school days.

Maxine bit her lip and shook her head in disbelief. What did Darren want money for now? Twice she had helped him out by 'investing' in his dreams. It had been less about earning potential and more about reconciliation. She wanted to show him she could be a supportive mother, even if she hadn't been when he was growing up.

Two investment schemes and two disasterous losses. Being supportive of Darren was too costly for her peace of mine. After the second time, when he sent appeals for his latest scheme, she wrote back thanking him for thinking of her, but unfortunately, her financial planner had advised against supporting the project.

She sighed. She didn't have the time or energy to deal with Darren right now. Without reading the letter, she threw it on the nightstand and clicked off the light.

Maxine tossed and turned for an hour. *Screw this,* she thought. *I want to spend the night with my dad.* Within minutes, she was standing at the hospital door buzzing to get in again.

- - - - -

The chair in the hospital wasn't terrible to sleep in, Maxine thought, if you didn't have a bone in your body or muscles that would ache in the morning. She sat up and rubbed the back of her neck. Her whole body felt as if someone had taken a sledgehammer to it.

She glanced over at the hospital bed. Her dad's eyes were still closed, and the machines were beeping comfortingly. Maxine only wished that she felt as comfortable.

She bent to pick up her purse and was startled when something fell to the floor.

It was the stained letter she thought she'd put on her nightstand. For some reason, she must have transferred it to her purse when she'd been rushing out of the Lodge last night, sleepless and tired.

Well, she didn't feel any less tired, but she was certainly awake enough to deal with this. She unfolded the papers and began reading.

Dear Mom, the letter began. *I'm glad to hear that you're back at Laurel Lake. I just returned also, and heard from Daphne that Grandpa is in the hospital. I'll be visiting him tomorrow with her.*

Maxine snorted. She might not have been cut out to be a mom, but those two had never been good as brother and sister either. Maybe it was something that ran in the family.

The letter continued. *I want to tell you that we've had an amazing find. Remember that painting we all hated? That one Daphne sent to auction? The art appraiser looked all over the building, and it turns out there are more by Savario and his group all over the Lodge! There were eight in the storage room alone. They're worth millions! We're going to create a gallery space here in the Lodge, featuring these paintings, and it will be a monumental draw.*

Maxine gasped. Holy hell, did she read that right? She read it again, just to be sure, but the number hadn't changed.

The gallery will put Laurel Lake on the map, Darren wrote. *I had a wonderful idea about an investment opportunity in retirement homes . . .*

Maxine skimmed over Darren's pitch about his latest harebrained scheme. The only surprise when she read to the end of it was that he didn't ask her for money. A cynical part of her brain told her it was because he was trying to hit up his sister for a chunk of change from the sale of the paintings, but a smaller part of her thought maybe he was really interested in Laurel Lake at last.

Darren had followed in Maxine's footsteps and run as far away as he possibly could from the place, and she couldn't blame him for that. She knew how stifling this life had been for her.

But now she wondered—had she been so fed up with her marriage that she hadn't seen the forest for the trees? Perhaps there had been a hidden value in the old place this whole time, and only Duke had seen it.

She certainly hadn't.

If Daphne and Darren were able to work together to make Laurel Lake Lodge viable again, she had to applaud their commitment.

Good for them, she thought. *Good for them*.

"Maxine?" a quavering voice said.

She glanced up from the letter and felt it drop from her suddenly nerveless fingers.

Her dad's eyes were open. He was looking at her in full awareness.

She brought both of her hands to her mouth, stunned. Her eyes filled with grateful tears. "Dad!" she exclaimed, reaching out to clasp his hands in hers.

There was a ghost of a smile on his lips as his fingers returned a slight pressure against hers. "I heard you gasp— you woke me up," he said slowly.

Darren's letter, she realized. She knew that for some

inexplicable reason, that letter had brought her father back to her. And she was grateful for it, no matter what happened next.

30.
Dedications

Jonathan

Jonathan "Eddie" Edwards sat at the desk in Room 306. He was determined to fulfill his promise to Aggie. Maxine had taken him into the city and he'd seen his doctor. He had a prescription. He was taking control of his grief and his mental health. Moving forward didn't mean he was forgetting Aggie; it was honouring her.

He was committed to getting his novel written come hell or high water.

The computer monitor lit up. The cursor blinked at the first page of his manuscript. Where to begin? With Agnes, of course. He centred the cursor and typed.

I dedicate this work to Aggie,
without whose encouragement, quintessence, and
guidance, it would not exist.

Then he advanced to a new page, typed *Acknowledgements* and wrote,

I extend my gratitude to Darren Laurel ensuring our suite, our respite, our Avalon was expressly reserved every spring and summer.
I remain, with the profoundest veneration, your faithful

servant,
Jonathan M. Edwards.

He read it over. He could hear Aggie laughing, "Pretentious, much? Oh, Eddie." He smiled at the thought. Then he advanced to a fresh page and began to type.

After several hours, a noise interrupted his concentration. He scowled, trying to find his train of thought. Loud chatter outside his window erased it completely and he sighed, giving up. That would do for now. He saved the document, closed the file, and turned off the computer.

Pushing himself from the desk, he rummaged through the drawer and withdrew a thick writing pad and pen. He took a moment to open the curtains ("Let in the sun, Eddie. You're living like a mole!") and unlatched the window. The rusty hinges rasped and squeaked. No one had oiled them in a while.

He leaned his head out to see that the source of the chatter was a vanload of people stretching, gazing around, and moving toward the Lodge. Leading the way was a short man with dark hair, who gestured wildly and spoke loudly. It had been his voice which had interrupted Jonathan's intense writing. Jonathan scowled down at the man, but no one saw.

He knew with his concentration broken he would not get anything more written today, so he changed his clothing and put on his hiking boots. He tucked a pen and notebook into his jacket pocket. Perhaps a stroll around the lake would restore his concentration. If he was inspired along the way, he could record his ideas.

On the threshold of his room he turned automatically to tell Aggie he'd be back soon. His eyes had flicked around the room before he remembered, and the grief stabbed into his heart again.

Still. He could swear that he could feel her in the room. "I'll be back soon, Aggie," he said.

He imagined she replied, "That's fine dear, I'll just read until you're back."

He descended the stairs instead of taking the elevator. With each step he pondered the countless pairs of feet had gone up and down over the years.

When he emerged in the lobby he strolled past the many paintings, each depicting the landscape surrounding Laurel Lake.

Pausing beside one portraying a vivid sunset lighting the area in nearly glowing pinks and yellows, Jonathan leaned in to examine the small gallery tag on the wall.

He smiled as he read that it was Duke's own work, available for two thousand dollars. He knew the red dot meant it was sold.

Aggie would be pleased, he thought. She'd recognized Duke's brilliance years ago and had made a point to ask about his art each visit, encouraging him to paint more.

Jonathan was walking across the newly carpeted lobby toward the dining room when Christopher called out from the registration desk, "Professor Edwards!"

"Yes?"

"Daphne told me to watch for you. We have something that belongs to you." He reached down and then set a vintage hatbox on the desk. "This was left in your suite some time ago, with a note asking us to keep it safe for you until you returned. Grace came across it in a storage room during The Great Painting Search."

Jonathan's heart gave a lurch. "Thank you, lad." He accepted the box with unsteady hands and turned toward the dining room.

Celina welcomed him and, from across the room, waved him to his favourite table by the window.

After he settled in his chair, Jonathan studied the pretty box. He'd seen it before in his own hall closet at home, years ago. Aggie had stored the vintage hats she thought were so cute in them. He took a deep breath before he pulled off the lid. Pressurized air escaped with a whoosh. The scent thus released pushed him to the back of the chair. Aggie's gentle floral fragrance: jasmine and musk with the slightest hint of grapefruit. There was no doubt. She had left this box for him.

He removed the tissue paper to reveal the object nestled with such care and was instantly flooded with memories. He reached in and withdrew a cap from the box. Burying his face into the pristine linen fabric, he was swept back in time. He muffled a sob.

He could hear Aggie's voice informing him, "The Gatsby cap gives you an understated look."

He sat with an unfocused gaze, stroking his fingers across the stiff, narrow brim. He set the cap on his head and stared out the picture window. His reflection made him appear to be a ghost amid the trees. Oh, Aggie, I've been barely a phantom without you.

Celina set down a pot of tea and a mug. "I thought I'd get you started before I go on my break. Christopher is taking over for a bit. The special tonight is Salisbury steak with mashed potatoes and gravy. Would you like that?"

Jonathan nodded. "Yes, please. That sounds perfect."

"I'll give this to the kitchen, and then you can call Christopher if you need anything before I'm back, okay?"

Jonathan smiled. "I'll be fine. Thank you, my dear."

He was still staring out the window, lost in his thoughts, when there was a discreet cough at his elbow. He looked up to see Christopher, his hair flopping into his eyes, shifting from foot to foot with a tray of food in his hands.

"Professor Edwards," Christopher said, a scarlet wave rising from his neck. "Here's your dinner."

"Ah, yes. That looks delicious." In his mind he was still wandering around the lake with Aggie.

"I'm sorry, sir, I don't mean to be rude, but is everything all right?"

Jonathan blinked back the tears that flooded his eyes at the lad's kind concern. "This was my wife's favourite place in the world. She loved Laurel Lake any time of the year but now in particular." He gestured toward the lake. "She loved to walk around the lake. All the way around." He made a circle with his hand. He gazed back out the window, as though talking to himself, he continued, "She called this place 'Our Camelot.' It was here, in this very dining room, she lectured me about the fleeting nature of life, urged me to savour every moment."

Christopher was watching him intently.

"Truly, finding joy amidst the ache of Aggie's absence is arduous, but at Laurel Lake Lodge, her presence gently returns to me." He rested his fist against his heart. "I feel her here."

In his mind he heard Aggie say, "You're being pretentious again, darling." He could even feel the playful nudge of her elbow.

Christopher said, "I'm just so sorry you are going through this." He couldn't maintain his gaze into Jonathan's eyes.

"It's a lonely journey," Jonathan said, shifting in his seat. "But unless we are the first to depart this mortal plane, it is a journey we all will take." He could almost see Aggie roll her eyes at him. He sighed and shifted in his chair, glancing around the nearly empty dining room. There was just the regular from town.

He waved at the chair where Aggie should be sitting. "Why don't you sit for a moment, young Christopher. No one needs your attention at this moment."

Christopher scanned the room, and then nodded. "Just for a moment, I guess."

He removed a tightly rolled piece of paper from his back pocket and set it on the table as he sank into the chair.

"What's that?" said Jonathan, nodding at it.

"It's just a poster for a writing contest." Christopher rested his hand over the paper and the scarlet rose from his neck up to his cheeks.

Jonathan held out his hand. "Let's see."

Christopher pushed it across the table.

Jonathan unrolled it, putting a glass on the top and setting his knife across the bottom to hold it flat. He read the details, then leaned back in his chair, analyzing Christopher.

Christopher looked away as the scarlet hue moved into his hairline. "I should get back to work," he muttered, shifting his feet beneath him.

Jonathan put out a hand. "Wait a minute. Do you want to try to win this scholarship and attend university?" His tone demanded an answer.

"Ah, yes. But . . ." He closed his eyes. "I don't think my writing is good enough."

"It is my experience," Jonathan said, as he removed his knife from the bottom of the poster so it curled back to his glass, "that bad writers tend to think they're brilliant, while excellent writers tend to think they are mediocre."

Christopher blinked.

Jonathan tapped the poster with his index finger. "I believe that this would be an excellent opportunity for you. A full university scholarship is not to be sneezed at and besides, what do you lose by applying? You already don't have a full scholarship. If you apply, you may receive one." A smile lifted the gloom from Jonathan's face. "I can vouch for the university. I taught there myself until I retired recently."

Christopher bounced his right knee and stuttered, "I want to go to university. But my family can't afford it."

A couple came to stand at the 'Please Wait to be Seated' sign.

Jonathan nodded over to them. "It looks like you need to get back to work, but listen, I'd like to help you. We have enough time to meet the deadlines." He cut into his Salisbury steak. "We can start tomorrow if you like. When are you off work?" He lifted his water glass, and pushed the poster across the table.

Christopher grinned as he stood up and slipped the paper back into his pocket, "I have the dinner shift, so I start at four o'clock. How about early afternoon?"

"Two?"

"Perfect." Christopher strode across the dining room to greet the couple with a very definite bounce to his steps.

"My friends call me Eddie," Jonathan called out, as he turned his attention to his meal.

- - - - -

The next morning Jonathan picked up his canvas bag with its notebooks and pens and ambled down to the lake.

Standing on the lakeside trail, the waters stretched out before him. Leaves of the aspen, birch, and poplar trees swayed and fluttered in a graceful dance, whispering tree secrets about love and loss. The reflection of the mountains shimmered on the lake. Magnificent snow-covered summits loomed in the distance, ascending into the azure blue Alberta sky. The citrusy sharpness of pines filled the air. Despite the early hour, canoeists already paddled silently across the lake.

"*Solvitur ambulando,*" he said to the air. "It is solved by walking."

Jonathan pulled out his pocket watch and checked the time; it was eight o'clock. When had his watch started working again?

As he set it back into his pocket, he saw a familiar face striding along the trail.

"Maxine!" he exclaimed, and her head rose from its contemplation of the path in front of her.

She waved and hastened toward him. "Professor! I'm so glad to see you."

"How many times have I told you to call me Eddie?"

She just laughed. "How are you doing today?"

"Still missing my Aggie," he said. "She would have loved this beautiful day."

"She would. She was a beautiful soul." She looked around and inhaled the forest before she added, "But she was also a smart woman. She is here still, you know. In your memories of this place, and the happiness you shared here."

Jonathan nodded, "Yes. I sense her here. This has always been a happy place for us. And how are you?"

Maxine suddenly seemed mesmerized by the roots and rocks at her feet. "It's not my happy place, that's for sure. But my dad is doing much better. He's been moved out of the HDU into a regular unit. But how's your book?"

He laughed. "Forty pages yesterday, can you believe it?"

"That's wonderful. I know Agnes believed your writing is a great gift to the world. I know she would be delighted you're being an inspiration to others."

"How kind."

"Eddie, I'm serious. I saw Christopher last night. He told me what you offered to do for him. Agnes would be so happy about that." She took a step to the side, to continue past him on her walk. "I'm glad the book is finally really coming. I look forward to being at your book launch. Aggie would be so happy!"

It was true, Jonathan thought as he sat on Savario's memorial bench, watching the birds soar around the lake. Aggie was still here with him. While he could not hold her or love her as he had before, he could feel her love surrounding him.

And he knew that love would last his lifetime.

31.
Changes

Darren "Duke" Laurel Sr.

Duke dreaded the early morning light that stubbornly resisted the black-out curtains of his bedroom. Four-thirty in the morning and enough light was already seeping in around the window to illuminate his single bed, the armchair, a small desk, and a shelf cluttered with an assortment of art supplies he needed to take up to his studio on the fourth floor.

Once, Duke had loved early mornings. Getting up before anyone else in the Lodge was awake, sitting on the deck with his first mug of steaming black coffee, he could savour the stillness of the lake, the way the sun's rays slanted in almost sideways, the way it gave the world an ethereal quality.

It was a moment of peace before Leeroy arrived to hear the day's tasks or before he went to check on the kitchen to ensure things were prepared for those guests who also appreciated an early start.

On the day would roll, as he did repairs, checked on staff, ordered supplies. It was growing crescendo of activity until the stillness of night finally returned in the late hours.

But now he was stuck in his room with nothing to do. No responsibilities.

His muscles and joints were too weak and

uncoordinated to do much yet. At the hospital they'd said his physio-therapy sessions would help, but progress was slow and he didn't like being helpless.

He'd been surprised to see that Daphne seemed to be doing all right running the Lodge in his stead. She was changing things, though.

He thought about the new computer registration system that he didn't understand and glared through the wall to where the evil device had replaced his guest registration book that had worked perfectly well for decades. Change was coming. The lodge would never be what it was.

Duke closed his eyes for a moment, willing himself to fall asleep again and escape this empty room and the mocking light, but his damned bladder was too full. He sighed and carefully swung his legs over the edge of his bed. He fumbled for his cane and tottered across to his bathroom.

Moments later, his bladder relieved, his hands washed, and his stubble shaved away, Duke hobbled over to the small chest of drawers beside the door. He fished out a clean undershirt and socks and tossed them onto the bed, then he grabbed the brown corduroy trousers and green plaid shirt he'd worn yesterday. He tossed them over to the bed as well, then shuffled back to the bed himself to sit and get himself dressed.

It was his suite behind the registration desk, but if he wasn't needed to man the desk, would it be better for Daphne to stay here? He could maybe move into his art studio on the fourth floor. He wasn't going to be taking those stairs any time soon, but the elevator worked. Most of the time. He should see when it was due to be serviced next. Daphne should check on that.

Of course, being on the ground floor meant hearing more of the hustle and bustle as staff and guests moved in and out of the lobby and dining room. Hustle and bustle that he was no longer part of.

He looked across to his calendar. On the fifteenth he'd written *Scout 1 p.m.*.

Ah, well, Duke thought, as he snapped the last clip of his suspenders. *Not much longer now.*

Duke stood up, grasping his cane, and made for the door. The clock on his nightstand read 5:13. Maybe that new cook would be in the kitchen already and would have coffee ready.

The chef was not in the kitchen. Duke let the kitchen door swing shut and turned away in disgust. Why was he the only one up so early?

The lodge was silent and still. It was summer and the Lodge was full of guests, between the families enjoying freedom before school started again, and folks who'd found them after those tour groups' posts 'went viral,' whatever that meant. A full lodge should mean someone would be around early in the morning, but no one was in the lobby yet, not even the staff.

Eddie would be down soon, Duke thought. *Eddie was a morning person too, right?* Duke suddenly couldn't remember. Maybe Agnes had been the morning person.

Duke needed his morning coffee, but since he had scalded himself on that fancy new hissing coffee machine

Daphne and the new chef had installed in the dining room, he'd been banned from making his own.

Duke sighed and shuffled across the lobby. This was a new part of his routine, wandering around to observe what had changed and to try to recognize what remained the same. He probably should have told Daphne that he'd arranged to sell the Lodge. Here she was, wasting money fixing things up when new owners would probably redo everything.

On the other hand, he didn't want to hear her objections. It was done. Darren had always made it clear that he didn't want the Lodge. Daphne was a girl and running the Lodge was no business for a girl, regardless of her fancy-pants degree.

He had to admit, though, she had been holding things together surprisingly well while he was recovering. Still. Women were unreliable. They didn't stay around.

He looked around the room. The wallpaper in the hallway was the same, the faded but sober, regal blue-green pinstripe, but the carpet was new, a charcoal grey with a pale border. The art on the walls was a mix of pieces Duke had collected for the Lodge over the years, a few of his own work, and newly, a few contemporary prints that Daphne had selected. He didn't think he liked them, but maybe they'd grow on him.

In the dining room it looked as if time had stopped. The morning sunlight streamed in through the large picture window that framed the glacial blue lake beneath the looming, snow-capped mountains.

On the wall just outside the dining room, a large map was tacked up on a bulletin board, showing all of the hiking trails in the area, along with an assortment of posters, business cards, and menus for local events and businesses. He noticed there was a new security camera tucked into the upper far corner. Duke scoffed at the waste of money that represented. As if there was ever going to be trouble here! Their clientele were not troublemakers.

Inside the dining room, Daphne had replaced the tables and chairs with ones that 'had a rustic Nordic vibe,' as she put it. Duke didn't know anything about Nordic vibes, but he had to admit that the pale birch veneer and straight-backed chairs looked attractive. The dining room was too empty, though. Where was the new chef? And where was Eddie? Or anyone else? Had everyone been raptured? No, he didn't know anyone pious enough to have been raptured. He wondered if he should pull the fire alarm and wake everyone up. But no. There was a five hundred dollar fine for a false alarm. He couldn't afford it.

Walking through the dining room, Duke used his master key to slide open the glass doors and stepped out onto the terrace. The air was brisk, smelling of earth and trees and lake water that now seemed too cold nowadays for him to swim in. The kids still did, as he had in his youth. Maybe kids just had more fortitude.

He settled into one of the deck chairs and admired the small beach and floating dock. How often had he pushed out small Darren and Daphne in their canoe onto the lake from just that spot? They could never seem to paddle together, so they always lurched and spun until they were both sputtering and squealing in the water.

He looked at the canoes and paddle boards pulled up for the night and recalled the moonlit paddles with Maxine when they were first married and so much in love. Bah. Love. What a waste of time and energy that had been.

As the water gently lapped the shore, he remembered evenings sitting on this terrace with his parents. He glanced up at the sun; it was a little higher in the sky now, but still shining sideways through the crystal clear morning. He yawned.

All of this is what he loved, had given his life to, and all of this would end.

Soon.

Too soon.

Duke closed his eyes and leaned back into the chair, wishing that the stroke had killed him instead of leaving him crippled and too weak to face the future.

"Good morning!"

Duke startled awake and squinted blearily up to see Eddie beaming down at him.

"I said, Good morning!" Eddie boomed.

Duke wasn't that deaf, was he? Duke looked around, realized he was sitting on the terrace. The sun was higher above the horizon. How had he fallen asleep when there was so much to do?

But no, he caught himself. There was not much for him to do anymore.

Eddie held two steaming mugs of coffee and carefully

set one in front of Duke. "I thought you might be ready for your coffee."

"Thanks." Duke leaned forward in his chair and lifted the mug with his more steady hand.

Eddie sat down in the chair next to him, and stretched out his legs. "I can never get enough of this view," Eddie declared. "Just look at those mountains. The greens are magnificent, the darker spruce and pines mixing with the aspen and birch. And then the stark grey and sharp lines of the rock above the tree line, like someone shaved off chunks with a knife. And then that gorgeous white snow on top. Still now, even in August. And all of that reflected in the lake. What a treat to sit here and take it all in. It's like a painting."

Duke took a sip of his coffee. It was hot and black. He had to admit Daphne's coffee was better than the pre-ground stuff he used to buy for the Lodge. He always had chosen the cheapest coffee he could get from the restaurant supplier. Maybe that had been a mistake. He stared out at the lake and mountains and felt the sun warming his skin. "It sure is a good view," Duke agreed, wistfully. "And it's certainly been painted, plenty. As you well know."

"You say that like you don't expect to see this view for much longer," Eddie said. "Is anything wrong?"

"No, no, nothing's more wrong than yesterday," Duke replied. "Some things don't last forever. I guess I'm feeling my mortality."

"Ah, yes. Since I lost Agnes, mortality has been on my mind, too. You and I certainly won't last a century or two," Eddie replied, "but I suspect this view will." He raised his mug in a salute to the beauty around them. "I'm thankful for it and for you making this lodge so welcoming."

Duke snorted noncommittally and thought of his discussion with the land developer and those documents he'd signed. Eddie didn't need to know about that any more than Daphne did. He'd find out soon enough.

The men sat together in companionable silence, drinking their coffee and letting their eyes linger over the trees and the peaks, watching the birds hunt for their breakfast, and admiring the way the breeze rippled the surface of the water.

"So what are you going to work on today?" Eddie asked, after he set his empty mug on the table between them. "I was impressed with that landscape you painted last week."

Duke snorted. "That was a failure. Not even a good study for a real painting." Duke thought back to his art studies, fifty odd years ago. That was real art. His instructors would be ashamed to see his efforts now with his trembling strokes and crooked lines.

Eddie broke through his thoughts. "Ah, don't be so hard on yourself. Not on such a beautiful morning. So you are not going to be part of the Group of Seven. So what? You capture what you see. Anyway, I'm hungry. Are you coming for breakfast?"

Duke let Eddie's comment slide. "Sure. About damn time."

Breakfast over, and the clock already ticking toward ten o'clock, Duke shuffled back to his room to retrieve his sketchbook and then wandered back over to the lobby. There was a buzz to the Lodge these days, he thought. A young family tromped through on their way out the front door, kitted out for hiking. A murmur of voices and clattering dishes came from the dining room.

Daphne stood behind the registration desk, doing something on the computer. She looked up as Duke went by and smiled brightly. "Morning, Dad! How are you feeling today?"

"Fine." Duke stopped in front of the desk, placed his sketchbook on top. "What do you have planned?"

"Well," Daphne replied, glancing back at the computer screen, "I'm meeting with the carpenter at ten to discuss refurbishing the rooms on the third floor. We'll start that in September, once the off-season starts."

"There's no need for that," Duke muttered. He should tell her he'd sold the Lodge, but he didn't have the energy to face her reaction. "Don't trouble yourself."

"It's no trouble. I'm just doing my job." She smiled at him. "This afternoon I'm meeting with another tour operator. Maybe we can get more business during the winter months. Oh, and I've been talking with Maggie from the Arts Society. She suggested we could help host some kind of winter wonderland that will draw visitors and help everyone in town. There is so much untapped potential here."

"You didn't think you should consult me about any of this?"

Daphne didn't reply, but she looked at him with disappointment radiating off her.

If she was disappointed now, how was she going to react when she found out he was in the process of selling the Lodge? It was his to sell though. He hadn't even agreed to hire her. If she was working under some misapprehension, that was on her. Duke sighed and took a couple of steps toward the door.

"What were you planning to do today, Dad? More sketching?"

Duke stopped. He'd forgotten about the sketchbook. He turned and grabbed it off the desk. "I guess," he said.

"What are you going to sketch?"

Duke shrugged. "Still life of fruit bowls is boring. Animals move too fast. People are so damn complicated. I can't get my fingers to stop shaking enough to hold the pencil properly."

"You are improving," Daphne said. "I think this art therapy is really working. And you do like art, right? You told me you did in the hospital, remember?"

"It was a moment of weakness," he muttered. He shouldn't have told Daphne about his long-lost dreams to be an artist. Ah, to be at the art institute in Calgary again. Oh, for those summers spent painting watercolours and oils out in the fresh air with the amazing instructors at the Banff Centre. He'd been going somewhere back then. He was supposed to have a show. And then his dad had to fall off the damn roof and break his back. There was no longer time for art. The lodge became his all-encompassing responsibility.

Daphne laughed, "Weakness or not, I'm thankful you told me."

Duke grunted. "Just because I liked it once doesn't mean that I'm any good at it these days."

"Oh, Dad. I have always thought your art was wonderful," Daphne said. "Your taste is impeccable. You added to the collection your parents began with their artist retreats from the early days, right?"

"Yeah, I suppose."

"I understand it's frustrating when you're out of practice and the stroke is messing with your eye-hand coordination, but you're getting better every day, Dad. Please keep it up."

Duke harrumphed, but fought a smile at the idea that Daphne had actually liked his artwork when she was growing up. In his memory she'd been a surly and solitary figure who hadn't liked much beyond whatever book she was reading. Though, come to think of it, she had also done every job in the building at one time or another.

He looked out the doors. "I still don't know what to draw, though. Nothing is speaking to me."

Daphne thought a moment. "You like this lodge," she said. "Why don't you try doing some studies? Could you find little details to sketch, and then we could look through your sketchbook together so you can tell me all about them?"

"Yeah, that's an idea."

Leeroy walked into the lobby then and Daphne waved him over. "Help Duke with his painting stuff, would you? He's going to need a chair and his portable easel."

The phone rang. As Daphne reached to pick it up, she said, "Have a fantastic day. I love you."

Duke waved his hand in acknowledgment, as behind him Daphne said, "Laurel Lake Lodge."

He wondered when he'd last heard anyone tell him they

loved him. Years. Maybe decades.

After some wandering around, and surely distressing several of the guests wondering what was happening, Duke finally chose a spot.

Leeroy set down a folding chair and an easel he'd fetched from the attic. They argued like old times as Duke arranged things to his liking. "Shoo," he finally told Leeroy. "Go tick some of those chores off Daphne's mile-long list. Leave me be."

He set the sketchbook on the easel and began to draw a close-up study of a canoe at the dock. Later, he waved Grace down and had her help move his things to the edge of the forest, where he sketched his favourite sitting stump.

Leeroy brought him a sandwich and some coffee at lunchtime and helped him relocate to the roadside so he could capture the signpost at the end of the driveway.

As Duke sketched, he pondered his whole life had happened here, except for those few years studying. He'd grown up here, doing any task his parents needed help with. By the time he was a teen, he'd changed sheets and laundered them. He'd served in the dining room and cooked in the kitchen. He'd changed lightbulbs and rewired lamps. He'd taken reservations, carried bags, and helped find lost kids. He'd cleaned canoes and cleared trails. He'd known every inch of this property before he was a man, and then his dad had fallen off the roof.

If becoming a man means being responsible, his father's fall was the moment that made Duke a man. He'd taken responsibility for the Lodge and everyone working there.

They were like an extended family. Having the care of them had held him together after Maxine's betrayal. Somehow in the stress of the last couple of years, he'd forgotten how much he loved this place and the people here.

But times changed. Darren wasn't interested in his legacy and Daphne, well, she was getting married, she said. She would eventually have children who needed her and she would leave. So what other option did he have?

He flipped through his sketchbook and pondered that knowing he'd soon be leaving definitely didn't make recording these images any easier.

One moment he thought it was better to forget that the deal was in the works and that he'd be signing the final sale papers any day now.

The next moment, he thought it was better to remember. At least drawing the Lodge he'd have captured some of the little things he wanted to recall, painful as the images would likely be to look at when he lived elsewhere.

In the following days Duke continued his practice of wandering inside and out, but now he looked with a renewed aesthetic purpose. He looked not as an an owner, searching for maintenance needed, but as an artist, searching for beauty in small things. The vista was glorious, but it was obvious. Once he was looking, he found so much beauty hiding in plain sight.

He studied the ridge line of the roof. He noticed how the roof curved and intersected with the walls. He looked for the lattice work that framed the windows and balconies. He looked for the traces of scrollwork which decorated the inside of the Lodge, near windows and doors, relics of a bygone era, most carved by his father. A few carved badly by himself, or even more poorly by Darren. The ornate bell on the reception desk. The swirl on the feet of a claw-footed tub. So many lovely little things to notice.

On the third day, Duke laboriously climbed the three flights of stairs to the attic, his strong hand gripping the bannister, his weak one clutching his cane. Strong leg first. Then the cane. Finally the weak leg. Repeat.

"Mr. Duke, sir!" Christopher left the housekeeping cart and rushed up to him on the first floor landing. "You should take the elevator!"

"I'm fine. This is physio-therapy. Go away."

His sketchbook, along with a thermos of coffee, was stuffed into a fabric tote bag he'd borrowed from the chef. It swung and bumped against his legs as he climbed.

On the second floor Grace came out of a room and rushed over to him. "Is there something wrong with the elevator?"

"No," panted Duke. "This is physio."

She looked at him dubiously, and watched vigilantly from the landing while he continued his arduous climb, as if she were prepared to catch him if he came tumbling down.

Leroy was waiting on the third floor landing with his hands on his hips, disapproval and worry wafting off him like fumes.

Duke just glared at him and carried on without a word.

It took Duke nearly twenty minutes to climb to the top. He leaned over the railing and called down, "I made it and

I'm still alive!"

From the lobby Daphne snickered.

His attic studio was stuffy and dark. Duke shuffled to the windows and opened them wide to let in fresh air. They flooded the room with sunlight. He looked down at the lake and up at the mountains. It was all so beautiful. Then he turned a full circle while he considered his room.

Everything was coated in a fine layer of dust. Canvases leaned up against the wall opposite the windows. The shelves were stacked with canvases, various types of paper, and his notebooks.

He had a drafting table in the corner by one window and two easels marked with years of paint drops and smears in the middle. Duke walked over to the old armchair, and arranged it so he had a view of both the window and the door. He dragged an old side table over too, and placed his thermos and sketchbook on it, and then sat down. He sipped his coffee, composed the scene in his mind, picked up a 3B pencil, and then settled the biggest sketchbook onto his lap.

This is what he'd missed most while he was in the hospital, and this is what he loved about Laurel Lake Lodge.

Despite being a lodge full of people—if he were fortunate to have a full house—he liked having his own space. From here in the attic, he could look out onto his lake and the mountains, and feel like he was on top of the world. When the sketch was done, he closed the book and hauled himself up. He put that sketchbook away and picked up a little one.

Duke had been amused to discover that he enjoyed the

architectural drawing of his studies around the Lodge. He liked to settle himself in unexpected corners to sketch doorknobs and lintels and the curve where the walls met the ceilings.

He needed more coffee, so he decided to take the little sketchbook downstairs to the terrace.

He sipped a fresh cup of coffee and enjoyed one of Chef Leo's excellent scones.

"Hi, Dad," said Daphne. "What are you working on?" She looked over his shoulder and said, "Keep it up!" as she was summoned back to the lobby by the clear call of the bell.

Eddie sat beside him on the terrace and wrote in his his notebook while Duke drew.

"I've got a long way to go," grumbled Duke.

"I like them," said Eddie, peeking over at the page. "They really capture the character of the place."

"My straight lines are never straight and half the time the perspective is skewed. Look!"

Eddie just laughed. "Artists are as self-critical as writers, apparently. I think your work is charming. If you want photorealism, then you should take up photography."

Duke was so wrapped up with his drawing that he completely forgot it was the fifteenth. Today he had an appointment with the land developer.

32.
Sign here

Duke

Duke was sitting in his folding chair tucked under the trees at the end of the driveway with his sketchbook on the easel and a pencil in his hand, sketching out the curving lines of the road beneath the trees, when the crunch of gravel behind him made him turn around.

"What are you doing here?" Duke demanded.

Walking languidly toward him with a slight self-satisfied smile was Scout Pinson, the land developer. Duke glared at her.

Scout's smile deepened. "Hello, Mr. Laurel," she said. "It's good to see you. It's signing day. Our lawyer's waiting in the dining room."

"Signing day?" Duke repeated, his hand holding the pencil dropping forgotten into his lap.

"All the approvals have come through and the final documents are ready," Scout confirmed, stopping and leaning against a tree, as if she already owned the place. "I must say, this can't be the best view of the place. The lake is more picturesque."

"It's all picturesque," Duke retorted. He rediscovered the pencil in his lap, tucked it away in his shirt pocket, and snapped the sketchbook shut.

He felt angry at having forgotten this meeting and at having Scout, this smarmy woman, sneak up on him like that. And he felt a renewed wave of grief that his time at the Lodge really was ending soon and he would no longer have a home here and that his staff would all be out of jobs. And he felt ashamed that his time as steward of the Lodge had to come to this. He had given up on the property because he could no longer care for it. He had let down his parents' legacy. He squared his shoulders. It had to be done.

"How'd you know I was here?" Duke asked.

"The woman at the desk directed me. We drove right past when we arrived and didn't realize it was you. You're an artist?"

Duke ignored the question. "Daphne knows you are here?" Panic lanced through Duke.

"I don't think she knows why we are here," Scout replied with a smirk. "Don't worry. I won't give away your secrets. I take it you didn't tell anyone about the sale?"

"There was still time," Duke grumbled. "And it is my lodge."

Scout nodded. "For the moment." Scout reached out a hand. "Let's go sign those closing papers, shall we? Do you need some help?"

"I'm fine," Duke growled, wishing he didn't need the cane. "Let's go up to my studio," Duke said. "It's on the fourth floor."

Scout texted the lawyer where to go.

As they rode the elevator, Duke considered why he didn't want any witnesses to this betrayal. He was selling his parents' dream, his own fifty years of labour and devotion, and the affection of the staff and guests who returned faithfully.

He was thankful Daphne hadn't been at the reception desk when they went through the lobby.

Scout stayed right on Duke's tail. Duke could feel her presence, like a stalking lion, behind him. The lawyer, a mousy man with greying hair and rimless glasses, fell in behind Scout.

In Duke's studio, Duke sat in his armchair by the window while Scout pulled the drafting table out from the wall to make more space for all three to gather around.

As Duke adjusted it to a flat horizontal, he was suddenly certain that this was a mistake. He shouldn't be doing this.

Scout pulled out a paint-splattered stool and sat, leaving the lawyer to stand. The lawyer pulled papers out of his briefcase, and handed a pen to Duke. Scout pulled out an expensive-looking fountain pen. The lawyer showed them where to sign.

Duke felt like he was in a strange trance, as if his body were signing while his spirit floated above shrieking, *Don't do it!*

But he did.

Signatures here.

Initials there.

The lawyer summarized the significance of each. Scout scribbled her name in large, looping letters, a gleeful smile barely contained. Duke's was a quivering facsimile of his former firm, slashing signature. The other two scrawls he saw on the bottom of the pages were tidy in comparison.

"This property is sitting on some prime waterfront, Duke," Scout declared, putting her pen down. "I know you know it. It deserves something special."

Duke grunted, scribbled his name where directed again. "You said I don't need to vacate for another three months, right?" Duke said, putting his pen down and staring out the window.

"Three months until we take possession," Scout agreed, standing up.

The lawyer extracted a bank draft from the briefcase and handed it to Duke. "Here's the signing payment." Duke took the cheque, but set it off to the side without looking at it. It felt ominously like thirty pieces of silver.

The lawyer gathered the papers and put them back into the briefcase.

"I hope your daughter takes the news well. Could be messy if you wait until the last minute." She nodded at the cheque and laughed, "I imagine that should be sufficient compensation for any distress she might feel." Scout stuck out her hand. "A pleasure doing business with you, Duke."

Duke regarded the hand in silence, and looked out the window at the lake and mountains. "You can see yourselves out."

Scout and the lawyer left and Duke sat silently in his chair, staring at the copies of the documents that had been left on the drafting table for him.

His parents' legacy and his life's work gone, just like that.

His home and his business that he had dedicated fifty years to. The famous Laurel Lake Lodge that his parents had established and sacrificed for would likely be bulldozed for condos or whatever Scout and her cronies could wring the most money out of.

Duke knew Scout's type. He didn't trust a word she'd said about honouring the history of the place or about ensuring that the Laurel family legacy continued. What was the legacy to Scout?

For her it was all about the money. How absurd that because Duke had needed money he'd had to sell the Lodge. Now Duke had the money, at the price of everything he cared for. He was an O. Henry story.

Duke sat and stared out at Laurel Lake, his body feeling heavy and numb. The sun shifted higher in the sky and the room began to heat up, but Duke didn't bother opening the window.

A knock on the door snapped Duke out of his whirling thoughts.

Daphne opened the door and poked her head in. "Hi, Dad. Are you coming down to eat?" Her brow was furrowed with concern.

Duke turned his head to look at his bedside clock, winced at how stiff his neck felt. It was already five o'clock.

"Sure," Duke said heavily. "I guess I lost track of the time." He reached for his cane and slowly pushed himself up.

"Is everything okay? Who were the people who came to see you?" Daphne asked.

"Nobody," Duke lied. "Nothing important."

He knew he needed to tell Daphne sooner or later about the sale of the Lodge, but now was not the right time.

- - - - -

Duke woke with a pounding headache the next day. Tylenol did little to relieve the pain. After a coffee, some eggs, and toast in the dining room, Duke retreated to his room and stayed in bed.

The lake outside seemed to match his mood. There was a stiff wind blowing whitecaps and a storm was forecast. The looming black clouds were as ominous as the feeling in his chest.

Daphne stopped in periodically to bring him tea and soup, which made Duke feel guilty. He glanced nervously to the drawer where he'd hidden the sale documents underneath his shirts.

Duke felt a little better the next day and sat out on the terrace, bundled up as if the fall had already arrived. He had his sketchbook with him, but he didn't feel like drawing.

Eddie came and sat with him for a short while, gazing companionably out at the lake, but wisely keeping silent.

Duke knew he would have to begin looking for a new place to live soon. He didn't think Daphne had room at her place in the city, and besides, he wasn't ready to fully give up his independence.

The third day dawned clear and bright, the sun waking Duke up early, as usual. Duke lay in bed, listening to the birds chatter outside his window. The sound made him smile, and he hoisted himself up to totter to the bathroom and then to get dressed. He still had two months and three and a half weeks before Scout's people took over, right? Better make the most of it.

Duke resumed his early morning tour of the Lodge, slowly making his way through the halls and common rooms on the main floor while everyone else slept. He stepped out onto the deck, and then walked down to the beach, spying ducks bobbing on the water and diving for their breakfast. He stood on the edge of the sand, both hands firmly planted on his cane, and closed his eyes. He drew in a deep breath, let it go. The cool breeze on his face reminded him that Laurel Lake would always be home, even if he couldn't always live here.

After breakfast, Duke sat in the lobby and sketched. He drew the front desk and this time, for the first time, he tried including people. He drew Daphne as she stood at the computer and as she assisted a young couple asking for advice on canoe rentals. He drew Grace as she came up to the desk to ask a question about something on her list. He drew Leo in his chef whites, in from the dining room to confer with Daphne about the menu. He drew Leeroy listening earnestly as she added to his maintenance list.

Looking back through his sketches, Duke still wasn't satisfied by his efforts to draw people. People moved too much, and his hand still wasn't steady enough, but there was an improvement. He had captured faithful likenesses of each of them. Duke sighed, reached for his coffee on the side table, and realized the mug was empty.

"Ready for lunch?" Daphne asked, coming up beside

him with a little smile on her face.

"I guess so," Duke replied. In truth, he didn't really feel hungry.

"I'm ready for lunch too," Daphne said. "Christopher's got the front desk. Come on, I'll join you. I have news."

She held out her hand to help Duke up.

Duke accepted, surprised. "Do you have time to take lunch? Don't you have work to do?"

Daphne smiled. "I think I can afford to have the occasional lunch with my dad. The lodge isn't going anywhere."

Duke winced at that, but he forced a semblance of a smile as he mumbled, "I guess not."

They made their way to the dining room, Duke leaning on his cane. Daphne carried his sketchbook slightly ahead of him.

"Okay. I can't wait to tell you," Daphne said, spinning to face him. "I've quit my job in the city. I'm going to come work here fulltime."

Duke made a gutteral noise and Daphne threw up her hands. "No. Wait. Don't say anything. I know you think women can't run hotels, but I've been doing it, Dad. Things are going well. The dining room is getting busier. People love Chef Leo's food. The repair schedule is going smoothly. Our bookings are growing. I want to see it through. Please?" She pulled him forward again.

'Uh," said Duke, his mind racing.

Now they had reached the dining room and Daphne stepped back, and—

"Surprise!" The dining room erupted with cheers and a rousing rendition of "Happy Birthday to you!"

Duke stood in the doorway, his eyes wide and his mouth agape, both hands clutching the head of his cane as he gazed around the room. Everyone he knew, it seemed, was crowded in. All of the staff, friends from town, even some of the regular guests, and was that Daphne's old boyfriend who had the railing business now? He blinked over at Daphne. "You planned a birthday party for me?"

"Happy birthday, Dad. Of course, we'll throw a party for you." Daphne leaned over and kissed him on the cheek. "This has been some year, eh? And you are doing amazing, adjusting to all of the changes."

"Well, perhaps," Duke said, flattered. "Thank you. How on earth did you sneak all these people in here while I was sketching in the lobby?"

"We used the terrace doors," Daphne laughed.

Celina stepped over. "We thought you'd surely notice, but you were so wrapped up in that sketchbook you saw nothing!"

Eddie stepped out from the crowd, arms wide for a hug. "Duke, my friend! Many happy returns! I'm so happy I can be here. I have something to show you."

Duke let himself be led forward by Eddie.

He spotted Grace, who stood beside her mother's wheelchair on the edge of the room, and gave them a wave. The two of them grinned and waved back.

Louise had worked for years and he didn't think he'd ever properly thanked her for her wonderful service. He must do that today. Grace was proving to be equally invaluable. He had certainly had wonderful staff over the years.

Eddie chattered away. "You do such a wonderful job with the art in this place, and I thought to myself, 'Eddie, who else is here that has such talent but is not represented on these walls?' and I thought of you! So come, my friend. I resolved the omission." With a flourish, Eddie gestured to the daisy-yellow wall and Duke gasped.

"That's my painting," Duke said. "The watercolour I painted of the lake, from the desk." Duke looked down the wall, and then turned around. "And there's that damned still life, and one of my sketches of the upstairs window."

Duke turned to Eddie and said, "You didn't."

"I did!" Eddie crowed. "Such talent should not go to waste."

"But most of these pieces are junk!"

Duke looked around the room again, and spied a pedestal in the middle of the room upon which sat a misshapen clay pot, which Duke recognized from art therapy class over the winter. "Where did you get that? I hate pottery. Could never get my hands to coordinate and mold the clay properly."

"Ah, my friend." Eddie took hold of Duke's hands and leaned in to look Duke in the eyes. "Not everything on display here is a masterpiece, I know. But it is all part of the journey—of *your* journey, and we are here to celebrate it! And if some pieces are so ugly they make us laugh, all the better!"

Eddie gave Duke's hands a squeeze and then let go.

"Come! I want to show you all the pieces I put up. And you should thank Daphne, too. Most of these would have been lost, I know, if not for her."

Duke hobbled along behind him as Eddie chattered away. It took a long while to navigate the room, as people approached to wish him a happy birthday and to chat. At some point, Leo brought out a freshly baked chocolate cake and Duke had to blow out the candles and make the first cut. He ate the first slice, as he sat at a table in the middle of the room, beside that hideous, deformed pot. Eddie was right, Duke had to admit, it was funny to see something so hideous elevated to fine art.

Leeroy brought him over a sandwich. "Are you hungry, Mr. Laurel, sir?"

"I am, thank you, Leeroy." It was tuna salad. His favourite. "Leeroy, did I ever tell you how proud I am of you?"

"Oh, sir!" said Leeroy. His face flamed red and he lunged out of the room.

"Too much," Duke murmured to himself. "I should have been a bit more subtle."

Duke sat back, chewing his sandwich, temporarily spared someone talking to him, and considered his future. Maybe he could be an artist again. He wouldn't ever show in galleries or become world famous, as he once dreamed, but maybe making art for himself was enough. He could continue to poke away at it and slowly improve. It would at least be something to fill the next part of his life, like the Lodge had filled it.

Another wave of guilt passed over him. He had to tell

Daphne he'd sold the Lodge.

"Hello, Dad," said a deep, jovial voice. "Long time no see."

"Good Lord," said Duke, choking as he tried to swallow a mouthful of tuna sandwich. "What are you doing here, Darren?"

"Didn't you hear? After Daphne turned up all the old paintings, we decided to team up to open an art gallery. I'm going to be the manager. I'm setting up appointments to meet with architects so we can choose the best site on the Laurel property and build something that perfectly suits the landscape. Cool, eh?"

Duke cleared his throat and reached for a goblet of some amber liquid. "Cool," he muttered, choking again, as it turned out to be neat whisky.

"We'll show your art, too, of course," Darren said with an expansive wave that encompassed the display.

"Huh," said Duke. "You don't have to do that."

"But I want to!" Darren said and began recounting all his ideas for the Laurel Gallery.

Duke scanned the room and spotted Daphne chatting and laughing in the corner with Maxine's father. That probably meant Maxine was the slender person with her back to him. That was all right. She could eat his cake. He had to talk to Daphne. Maybe if she acted quickly she could get her job back?

She laughed and leaned in to listen to something the person who was probably Maxine was saying.

She's too busy right now, he thought as a familiar cello

recording filled the room. *I'll do it another time.*

Molly beckoned at him from a chair by the window.

Duke didn't know how much longer he could put off telling Daphne, but right now was about celebrating.

"Excuse me, son," he said.

No one wanted to get bad news at a party, so he decided to go chat with Molly instead.

33.
Maybe not

Daphne

"You did what?"

Duke held up his hands as Daphne advanced on him, murder in her eyes. "I did what I thought was best," he told her.

But his voice wavered.

Daphne thought she knew why he was trying to present this as a done deal and why he hadn't told her about it before, but rage consumed her at his arrogance to make this decision without her.

"But . . . what about the Lodge? And everyone who works here? What about . . ." Daphne suddenly sniffed and wiped at her face. She was horrified to have tears come into her eyes. "Oh my god. I quit my job!" This was the worst thing that could have happened.

Duke reached out to touch her hand where it rested on his kitchen table, but she twitched it aside.

She could see the hurt in his eyes as she turned away from him, but he didn't deserve her sympathy, she thought. He was the one who'd disappointed her. Who'd disappointed everyone.

"I decided it was best. Your brother and you had shown no interest, and I'm not getting any younger."

Daphne threw her arms into the air. "No interest? How can you say I had no interest? I did a university degree in hospitality management and marketing. How is that no interest? I spent years managing hotels! How is that no interest? I've been running the place since your stroke. How is that no interest? I have coordinated tour groups and motorcycle groups! How is that not interest? I built us a website!" She shook her head, eyes blazing. "What planet have you been on that you didn't see that all that meant I was interested?"

"But you're a woman . . ." he started to say.

"I'm not even going to respond to any misguided misogyny or comments about Maxine. It's irrelevent, Dad. I'm not Maxine. I'm Daphne. And I love the hotel business!"

Duke stared at the floor, chastened. Everything she'd said was true. She'd done all those things, and he hadn't understood their significance. He'd been so blinded by his anger with Maxine he hadn't noticed that Daphne was a different person altogether, despite their physical similarities. "I'm sorry," he said. "I was stupid. I was completely blind and I see that I shouldn't have acted without consulting you, but I did. It's done."

"Dad," she said, her voice deadly calm. "You had no right to sign those papers."

"What?" His brow furrowed. "I know you don't like it, but I had every right to—"

"No." She shook her head. "You didn't have any right to, Dad. You weren't competent."

"Hey!"

"Remember how a few years back, you had your lawyer do the documents giving me enduring power of attorney in case you were incapacitated?"

"Yeah? So?"

"So, after your stroke, the doctors confirmed incapacity, so the EPA came into effect. That's why I've been able to run the Lodge. Right?"

He gave a slow nod.

"Since the EPA hasn't been revoked yet," she continued, "I'm the one who has to sign any legal documents on your behalf. You're still deemed incompetent. Sorry," she added, at his scowl.

"But . . ."

"When I was with you in the hospital, you told me to take care of things, remember?"

Duke's eyes widened. She could see him searching back in his memory, back to right after his stroke. When she'd had to make a lot of financial decisions and he could barely lift his head from his pillow. "By God, I did," he muttered.

"So I did. The doctors signed the incapacity and since it's not been rescinded, as far as the law is concerned, you had no right to sign those papers and sell off Laurel Lake Lodge."

Her triumph was short-lived as her dad was the one to blink rapidly now and look away.

"Incompetent," he murmured.

Despite him going behind her back and pulling the rug out from under her after all her work to turn the place around, Daphne's heart still ached for him.

He looked suddenly much older, almost frail. He'd aged a lot in the past year, and it was hard to reconcile the shrunken man in front of her with the robust man from her childhood who'd always seemed so strong and tough.

Her dad wasn't tough anymore. Far from it. He still walked with a cane to help him navigate the grounds, and the more she'd taken on, the less he'd attempted to do with the Lodge. But it was still his home. His legacy.

On second thought, perhaps his declining interest had had more to do with the fact that he knew the Lodge was for sale.

"Look," Daphne said. This time, it was she who reached out to put her hand over his. He welcomed her grip and she felt a pang in her heart over her petty action a few moments ago. "I know that you thought you were doing what was best for this place. But don't you see? This isn't the same lodge it used to be."

She ticked off points on her fingers. "We've painted the interiors and exteriors, renovated the rooms, reupholstered the worn furniture, and replaced the carpets. I've partnered with several tour groups, which have brought in a ton of business. Thanks to Leo, our restaurant is full almost every night. We're getting great reviews, which has brought our overall star rating way up." She raised her eyebrows. "If business continues at this rate, we can expand the walking paths around the lake and surrounding area next spring, as well as start offering boat rides and other guided activities. Maybe horseback riding in the future, or perhaps balloon rides. Darren's got the gallery project on the go, and I think this one will actually work out for him." She shook her head. "The sky's the limit, and I mean that both metaphorically and literally."

She could see her father was paying attention. "And, Dad . . . it's all working. The artists are interested in coming now there's going to be a gallery. Remember when I was a kid? Every winter, our place was filled with writers on retreats, artist groups coming through for a little winter magic, and families wanting a holiday away from home. We're booking through December now, and while we still have some space, I have a feeling this might be the first year in over a decade where we sell out for the month."

Duke took a deep breath, and she could see the considering look in his eyes. "Really?"

"Yes, Dad. Really."

Her dad seemed to sink into deep thought. He put his hand under his chin and slumped down in his chair. It worried her for a second—was he having another stroke?—until she realized he was just musing over everything she'd told him.

Surely, he'd noticed the changes for himself? He must have seen all the people in the lobby, the bustling activities in the rooms and dining hall, the people streaming in and out when before there had been nothing but crickets.

He glanced up at her, and she could see a new light in his eyes. "You," he breathed. "All this time, and I..." He shrugged his shoulders helplessly. "I should have listened to you years ago."

She remembered when she'd first gotten out of college and come back home for the summer. It had been her last season at the Lodge until Duke's stroke. She'd tried to persuade him to renovate, to expand, to reach out to other local businesses to grow their guest list.

But he'd turned down every single one of her suggestions. Until she'd given up for good and accepted the job offer that had been on the table at her graduation to work for one of the corporate chain lodges in Calgary. She thought she'd turned her back forever on the Lodge and what it had meant to her. To her family.

But in her heart she'd always felt the call of Laurel Lake. Where she grew up. She'd stopped calling it home a long time ago, but it had always been special.

However, she'd never felt her family thought that she was special. Her dad had always seen her as second best. Even when Darren showed no interest in the hospitality business, he was still considered the heir. He'd always put Daphne last, and she'd grown up feeling the sting.

"I was wrong," Duke said now. His voice was quavering. "Wrong about judging you." He passed a shaking hand over his face. "Wrong because I'm just a stubborn old man who can't see what's right in front of his face." He paused, then asked the question she'd been wanting to hear for so long. "Can you ever forgive me?"

But now that he'd finally asked it, Daphne realized that she didn't need to hear his apology anymore. While she'd always wanted her dad to realize her worth, it was enough for her to know who she was. It wasn't him she needed forgiveness from—it was herself. All these years, she'd put herself second, too. Not because she was, but because she felt that she didn't deserve first place.

With her father finally admitting his mistakes, she knew she didn't have to blame herself anymore.

She'd been holding herself back for too long.

It was time for her to let go of the anger and resentment she'd carried for all these years. It was time to start over.

Daphne stood up, and she came around the kitchen table to lean over her father and give him a hug. His arms rose to wrap around her back, and the two of them held that awkward embrace for what felt like a long, long time.

Finally, she pulled back, wiping again at her eyes. Two times in as many minutes! Man, she was getting soft.

But her own dad's eyes were wet too. If she was getting soft, he must be a marshmallow.

"Nothing to forgive," she told him. "I love you, Dad."

Duke took her hands and patted them, and then squeezed them for good measure. "I love you too, Daphne." He smiled waveringly up at her. "And I'm so proud of what you've done with the Lodge and I'm thankful that you have the ideas and the skills to make it thrive again. Thank you. I hope you can nullify the contract."

Daphne suddenly had another thought. "Dad, when you signed, where were you?"

"In my studio, why?"

"And who was with you?"

"Scout Pinson, her lawyer, and me. Daphne, what's this about?"

"Dad." She was nearly shaking now. "Who were the witnesses?"

"Sorry?"

"A legal document requires two witnesses to watch the parties sign. Who were your witnesses? You were there. Who else?"

"Me. Scout Pinson, Her lawyer. That's it."

"No one was there to watch you sign?"

"No."

Daphne pondered a moment. "Were there witness signatures on the documents?"

He tried to visualize the papers. Yes. There, beneath his signature, he could see it: two other scribbly signatures. Whosoever signatures those were, they hadn't been in the studio with him when he signed.

He shook his head. "They were already signed when the lawyer handed them to me."

Daphne grinned. "It'll be all right. Nothing about that contract is legal. I'll call our lawyer right now and everything will be voided."

"I'm sorry I made such a mess of things. And I'm sorry I didn't believe in you. You deserve to be running the Lodge. Let's talk to the lawyer about that, too."

- - - - -

"I know it's not what we planned," she said to Alex on the phone later that night. It had been an exhausting day—she'd spent most of it on a group call with Scout, her lawyer, and the Lodge's lawyer.

Scout had talked about suing for the broken contract,

but their lawyer had assured them that as long as the Lodge returned the funds that had been advanced to them, there wouldn't be a problem.

That was simple enough, as Duke hadn't taken the cheque to the bank yet.

The lawyers both agreed that the contract was null and void without Daphne's signature, and she made it clear that she would never sign.

Scout was fuming, but the deal was dead.

Duke made Daphne manager.

She was staying at Laurel Lake.

"I'm sorry," she told Alex. "I didn't expect this to happen."

"I know," Alex told her. His voice was heavy, and she wondered if this would be the final straw that broke her fiancé's back. He'd been infinitely patient with her the past year as she took care of her dad and ran his business, but she had told him for months that she was still planning on coming back to Calgary.

Both her grandfather and her dad were on the mend, and while Duke still refused to talk to Maxine, he'd mentioned her name the other day without flinching.

Small progress, but she'd take it.

Alex had visited her several weekends over the past year, and she'd even gone to Calgary a few times to visit him. But long-distance was a strain on any relationship, and they couldn't live in a separate town and city for the rest of their lives. It just wouldn't work.

"So, what can we do?" she asked, her heart feeling heavy. After such a wonderful breakthrough with her dad, she didn't want to have to say goodbye to the love of her life. But she couldn't abandon her dad either. She just couldn't.

"Tell you what," Alex said. His voice seemed distant. "Look out your window."

"What . . . ?" she drew back the curtains covering the window nearest to the bed.

Standing below was a figure. When he looked up, she could see his hand was holding a phone to his ear. The figure waved.

"Daphne," Alex said into her ear on the phone, and she could see his mouth moving below. "You know I love you. I'd follow you to the ends of the earth, but fortunately I don't have to go so far." His white teeth flashed against the darkness of his skin, and she held up a hand to press against the window. He held up one hand too, reaching out toward her. "I asked you to marry me, and I still want to, if you're willing."

"But . . . what about your career?" she asked, doubt in her heart. "I don't want you to give up being the director of a four-star hotel just to follow me to this small town."

"You're not listening," he scolded her with amusement in his voice. "I said I'd follow you anywhere. Even here." He moved his head from side to side, appearing to look around. "Besides, it's not so bad here. There's a certain charm about the lake. I felt it when I first visited you."

"Did you?" she asked, smiling.

He nodded. "So, what do you say? I could never ask you to give up your family or your dreams. But I can work anywhere with good internet. I'll have to go away for meetings now and then, but if you're here, Laurel Lake will be paradise to me."

Her mind raced back over the years. She considered how her mother had felt stifled here. Maxine had run away, leaving behind a bitter husband and two confused children who struggled for years to find their way.

But she wasn't her mom. And Alex wasn't her dad. They were themselves, and they didn't have to follow in her parents' footsteps. They'd find their own way, and it would be better than anything that had come before.

She smiled and put her hand to her mouth, blowing him a kiss that he would collect from her later that night. "Yes," she said. "I'd love that."

Please visit

LintusenPress.ca

to learn more about our upcoming releases

and to see submission calls

for future publications.

Thank you for leaving a review

on your favourite site or retailer

if you enjoyed this book.

HEAVENS TO MURGATROYD
Stories & poems

A fun collection of diverse stories and poems that *The Ottawa Review of Books* observes, "ranges from poetry to psychology, from genre to character study, from light to serious." Each piece features a character called Murgatroyd.

Contributors include Finnian Burnett, Zilla Jones, Robert Runté, Renee Cronley, Trent Lewin, Laurène Boutin, M. Gail Stelter, Donnalyn Rainey, Lindsay Harrington, T.L. Tomljanovic, Alma Lee, Lavinia Leon, Tom McCann, Robyn Diner, Shawn L. Bird, Trevor Hodges, Susan Duffield Lodge, Sherry Cassells and Janet Richards.

PLATYPUS TALES
Short stories celebrating the oddly unexpected

A quartet of stories celebrating the delightfully odd, from Finnian Burnett, Chris McMahen, Shawn L. Bird, and Janet Whitehead.

GHOSTLY
13 tales from beyond the veil

A collection of haunting short stories from Alix Kelinda, Finnian Burnett, Halli Reid, Jarrod K Williams, Jeanna Mason Stay, Kaitlyn Petry, L. N. Hunter, Lee F. Patrick, Leslie Wibberley, Marie Powell, Rob Nisbet, Shawn L. Bird, and Theric Jepson.

THE DRAGON PROBLEM
a collaborative novel

The village of Zos has a dragon problem.
Follow the townsfolk as they deal with an evil dentist, a decrepit dragon, a musical milkmaid, and political shenanigans.

A roomful of authors brainstormed this novel at When Words Collide Writers' Conference in 2023 and 10 authors worked together in subsequent months to craft this entertaining tale.

NEW SPACES:
an anthology of sci-fi short stories

Within your mind and across the universe, there are new spaces to explore!

From Lintusen Press comes this collection of ten science fiction short stories from authors Finnian Burnett, Andrew G. Cooper, J. Paul Cooper, BC Deeks, Nancy Kilpatrick, Philip Mann, Lee F. Patrick, Halli Reid, KT Wagner, and Jarrod K. Williams.

SMALL SHIFTS:
short stories of fantastical transformation

Not all shifters turn into magnificent beasts. Sure, there are those humans who transform into wolves and bears, but this book is about the smaller creatures. Learn about the trials and tribulations of folks who turn into raccoons, hamsters, mosquitoes, or bumblebees. 11 delightful tales of Small Shifts.

THE DRABBLE ADVENT CALENDAR

A drabble is a story of precisely one hundred words. Here are 25 family friendly winter themed drabbles; one perfectly complete tidbit of story to savour each day leading up to Christmas from authors Carol Parchewsky, Chris McMahen, Finnian Burnett, Lee F. Patrick, Shawn L. Bird, and Tim Reynolds.

Laurel Lake Lodge